THE FARMINGTON COMMUNITY LIBRARY
FARMINGTON HILLS BRANCH
32737 West Twelve Mile Road
Farmington Hills, MI 48334-3302

D0777110

SEP 15 2005

Clabbernappers

Clabber

STARSCAPE

A TOM DOHERTY ASSOCIATES BOOK
NEW YORK

30036009053388

nappers

✶ LEN BAILEY ✶

This is a work of fiction. All the characters and events portrayed in this novel
are either fictitious or are used fictitiously.

CLABBERNAPPERS

Copyright © 2005 by Len Bailey

All rights reserved, including the right to reproduce this book,
or portions thereof, in any form.

This book is printed on acid-free paper.

Map by Ellisa Mitchell

A Starscape Book
Published by Tom Doherty Associates, LLC
175 Fifth Avenue
New York, NY 10010

www.starscapebooks.com

Library of Congress Cataloging-in-Publication Data

Bailey, Len.
    Clabbernappers / Len Bailey.—1st ed.
        p.   cm.
    "A Tom Doherty Associates book."
    Summary: Eleven-year-old Oklahoma rodeo champion Danny Ray is sent to the
    kingdom of Elidor, where he sets sail across the Checkered Sea to rescue a kid-
    napped queen, despite the enemies found there and the dubious help of the prince
    and princess.
    ISBN 0-765-30981-5
    EAN 978-0765-30981-5
    1. Cowboys—Fiction.   2. Heroes—Fiction.   3. Pirates—Fiction.   4. Chess—
Fiction.   5. Kings, queens, rulers, etc.—Fiction.   6. Fantasy.   I. Title.

PZ7.B15258C1   2005
[Fic]—dc22

                                                                            2004057872

First Edition: February 2005

Printed in the United States of America

0   9   8   7   6   5   4   3   2   1

To Erika and Danny Gutt,
the most excellent,
the most neat,
the most cool grandparents
in the world

✵ Acknowledgments ✵

Any literary work is, in some way, inspired by earlier works and one's own life experiences. The seafaring otherworld of Elidor could never have been fashioned without my having been captivated by the excellent adventures of C. S. Forester's Horatio Hornblower and Patrick O'Brian's Jack Aubrey, nor could I have so enriched Elidor without having completely fallen under the magical spell of E. R. Eddison's *The Worm Ouroboros*. It was Mr. Laverne Steiner who instilled in me a love for God and for Oklahoma.

I have to especially thank two people for possessing amazing patience and insight: my agent, Tracy Grant, of the Leona Literary Agency in Northbrook, Illinois, and Jonathan Schmidt, senior editor at Tor/Starscape Books in New York.

For direction, advice, and friendship I am indebted to Charles and Karen Barrett; for a listening ear, to my godmother, Isabel Anders, and to Nancy Warmoth, Linda Wiebking, and Rose Kincaid. To Nancy L. Singer for peace of mind, and to Bob Roberts for encouragement. I must congratulate my youngest reader, Alex Bingham, for his fortitude. To the warmest, most loving teachers, Pam Yakel and Jackie Griffin, many thanks.

Lastly, but not least importantly, I extend thanks to the lovely women of the Wheaton Public Library, Wheaton, Illinois, for their encouragement and effort on my behalf.

Oh! And to Gordon Nielsen, my cabana boy.

❧ Contents ❦

Dragonfly Bay

Dumzil-
Daz

Checkered
Sea

Elidor

O alim el'iah ara
Ea eluim n'ara
'S hurim alim dlorimh h'alim
Ill uiem haluru alim 'ara

Dark is the Day, the Day of Doom
When shines no sun, shines no moon
A wind's age, a wolf's age,
Before the world's ruin

❯ 1 ❮
The Mumpokers

 POP!

A dart flashed in the sunlight and popped a red balloon. The young cowboy raised his fists in the air. His sparkling blue eyes squinted as he laughed and let out a shout. The boys and girls in line behind him hooted and hollered, the passersby at the Cherokee County Fair Grounds looking over with questioning glances.

"Seven balloons in a row!" said the proprietor behind the counter. "That ain't never been done—not while I been here!"

"What's my prize?" asked the cowboy, his red-and-yellow-striped shirtsleeves crossing. "Can I have that there stuffed red lizard?"

"Nope. That's a grand prize," said the man, shaking his head. He wore a Harley-Davidson vest and black T-shirt, and black gloves with the fingers cut off. "You gotta pop ten balloons in a row."

"Gimme some more darts!" said the cowboy, reaching in his pocket and putting down his last quarter.

"I'll bet you can do it!" chuckled the man, handing him

15

three more darts. His gray eyes fastened on the cowboy's large ornate belt buckle, which sparkled in the sunlight. "Champion calf roper, are you?"

"Bull rider!" said the cowboy proudly, pointing out the figure of a man on the back of a bucking bull. "But I'm still pretty good with a rope."

"Bet you are!" The man twirled his black beard around his finger. "I'll bet you could do darn near anything you set your mind to. What's your name, cowboy?"

"Danny Ray," he replied, fixing his stance and raising one of the darts.

But then the proprietor leaned over the counter and lowered his voice. "I got something a lot more exciting than that there red lizard." He motioned with his head to the side. "Yonder's a door you could walk through if you had a mind to it."

Danny Ray's blue eyes opened wide. His dart wavered, then lowered to the counter. Sure enough, there stood an open doorway with lightning flashing over its surface. Over the top was written this word: ADVENTURE.

"I ain't offered that to no one else before," said the proprietor.

Danny Ray glanced at the red lizard and then back to the doorway and asked, "What kind of ride is that? Looks mighty dangerous, with that lightning and all."

"Aw, that's just for show," the man said, waving his hand. "Of course, who knows what adventure's on the other side? Could be way too dangerous—even for a sharp young feller like you."

The cowboy licked the corner of his mouth and tasted a trace of cotton candy. He'd never met up with a challenge that he couldn't tackle.

"Just walk through that doorway, huh?" he asked.

"Yup," said the man. "Look. I'll send along a friend with you, a dazzling feller, to help you out of real hard scrapes, OK?"

Danny Ray looked around. "Where's he at?"

"You'll know 'im when you see 'im."

"Hmmm." Danny Ray hitched up his pants. They didn't really need hitching up, but it was a clear signal that he was considering undertaking an undertaking.

The proprietor ushered him around the counter and stood him in front of the doorway. Its shiny surface undulated like water. Now and then a bolt of lightning streaked across its surface.

"Hmmm," said the cowboy again.

He glanced back at the man, framed by the colorful hustle and bustle of the fair: flapping flags atop canopies, whirling whirligig rides against the backdrop of a pale blue sky, and the slow, ponderous turning of an immense white Ferris wheel.

"Guess I won't be needin' that lizard after all," said the cowboy.

"Here's your money back," the man said, handing him the quarter.

Danny Ray touched the rim of his hat in a polite gesture and then stepped through the doorway.

"Yeeeeee-hah!" yelled the cowboy as his feet went out from under him. He hung on to his hat as he fell into a lightning storm. Upside down he turned, or else his down side up was turned up side around, flopped over, and spun back down around again. It was like riding the fiercest, wildest bull ever, or else straddling the dark demon of a tornado. His leather chaps flapped wildly in the wind, and his spurs spun and sang! The wind blew his cheeks open as he dropped down into pitch blackness, like the open drain in a big bathtub.

The wind stopped.

The darkness lightened and Danny Ray felt the bottom of his boots come to rest against something solid. He found that he could stand, but he had to shield his eyes against a sudden bright light.

"Where the heck am I?" he muttered as a high rock wall and an ornate gate materialized.

The magic doorway had disappeared.

Nearby stood a line of statues of huge winged monsters, sparkling pink and red, each fashioned from a single gem. They lined a white-brick walkway leading to a vast palace in the distance, shining with crystal battlements.

"Wow!" he exclaimed, putting his hands on his hips. He felt something on his belt—a shiny, bright blue coil of rope. Mysteriously, his rapidly beating heart was calmed as he stroked the smoothness of it. So—this was his dazzling companion!

Something circled overhead, a tiny dragon no bigger than a sparrow, the same light blue color as the sky. It peered down upon him with red-jeweled eyes, and then shot away toward the palace.

Danny Ray saw a black centipede winding its way from the palace through the garden and along the walkway. As it got closer, the cowboy heard voices and could make out that the centipede was actually a line of small soldiers about two feet tall. Each of them was armored and helmeted in black and carrying a long black lance tipped with a sharp claw.

Shoot! Where could he hide? Behind him, towering above the wall and the trees beyond, a mountain range reached up to a terrible height. Danny Ray pushed against the gate's thick black bars, but it wouldn't budge.

"Some help you are!" he muttered, looking down at his rope.

Too late! The soldiers hustled quickly to surround him, lowering their sharp lances to almost touch him. The cowboy felt like the hub in the middle of a wagon wheel.

"Who the heck are you guys?" asked Danny Ray.

One of them stepped forward—presumably their captain, since he was wearing a badge. "We are the mumpokers!" he croaked. "The palace guards!" His glittering yellow eyes peered out from a kettle-like helmet pulled too far down on his brow. "We're taking you to stand before His Majesty King Krystal himself! Get going! No tricks!"

As they marched the cowboy toward the palace, now and then prodding him along with the points of their lances, the mumpokers chanted this song:

"Mum's the word!
Mum's the word!
Poke the parrot

And singing bird!
Hush the jabbering
That we overheard!
Shut your mouth
And mum's the word!

Mum's the word!
Mum's the word!
Kick the dog
And cat that purred!
Spank the ape
That yawned and stirred!
Mind your tongue
And mum's the word!"

Off to the side Danny Ray saw an avenue bordered by a row of black skyscrapers on one side and a row of white ones on the other. But wait! They weren't buildings—they were chess pieces!

"Wow!" muttered Danny Ray. "That's the largest chess set I've ever seen—ouch!" Danny Ray felt a jolt of pain as one of the mumpokers jabbed him in the rear end with his lance.

"Quiet!" said the captain, leveling a black-gloved finger at the cowboy. "Get marching!"

They arrived at the palace, and its immense pearl-white doors opened. As Danny Ray was poked for the one hundredth time and he yelled "Ouch!" for the one hundredth time, it came to him that a red lizard didn't seem so bad a prize after all.

✤ 2 ✤

The Dream Engine

 "The queen was kidnapped last night!" whispered Lord Yellow, tugging at King Krystal's shimmering white robe. "What if we're next? We should run away!"

But the old king, crowned in crystal and with eyes as clear as glass, frowned at him.

Lord Red, a short, barrel-chested man standing to the other side of King Krystal, bellowed, "Then run away, you soft-bellied, mealymouthed, slack-jawed, knock-kneed, teeth-chattering coward!"

Fire crackled from Lord Red's nostrils, but then he accepted a sparkling glass of cold cherrymaine from a passing servant resplendently dressed in white and gold silk and delicately balancing a silver tray. The servant disappeared into the humming crowd of great lords and ladies dancing to the accompaniment of harps and pipes, violins and cellos, tambourines, and the gentle tinkling of crystal glasses.

Lord Green sniffed, catching the scent of lavender swirling through the hall. He craned his skinny neck, like an ostrich, and leaned close to the king. "O King Krystal, most excellent ruler of Cherrydale, of Birdwhistle Bay, of Ironwood, and of all Elidor. Listen to my advice: We must pay whatever ransom is demanded for her!"

Lord Green felt a prickly pressure against his stomach and looked down at the prince, dressed in a black-and-white polka-dot robe, pressing the point of a sharp sword against him. "Then what about my treasure room filled with candy? What about my toys? What about my sword lessons? What about my—"

"What about putting your sword away, you little brat!"

"Curb your tongue, Lord Green!" cautioned King Krystal, reaching down and petting the prince's sprig of red hair. "You know how sensitive and sickly the lad is!"

"Sensitive, Your Majesty?" said Lord Red. "This same prince who glued my sword inside its scabbard?"

"Who poured punch into my violin?" said Lord Green with a frown.

"Who placed a blood buzzard's head inside my wife's wedding bouquet?" said Lord Yellow.

The prince screwed up his freckled face, smiled a wicked smile, and then grabbed a knuckleberry pastry off a nearby tray. He took a huge mouthful and began making an awful smacking noise.

Flip! Flip! Flip! In through the window flew the little dragon, circling over the surprised crowd and coming to rest on the king's outstretched arm. Instantly, its leathery hide turned snowy white to match the color of the king's robe.

Lord Red's glass of cherrymaine paused halfway to his lips,

and the prince crossed his arms and frowned. Lord Yellow let out a panicked howl.

"Ah, little gossip!" said King Krystal pleasantly. "What news, Scragtail?"

"Y'Majesty!" replied the gossip in a high-pitched croaking voice. "Has there happened something terrible—or something wonderful!"

"Catch your breath!" King Krystal stroked Scragtail under the chin with a curled forefinger. A low humming emitted from its open mouth, and its barbed tail rose and fell. "Stop your huffing and puffing and chuffing!"

"Has fluttered down into the main courtyard a shimmering square, like a giant blue leaf!" The gossip rolled its ruby-red eyes. "Wavers like a mermaid's hair, does it, with lightning streaked. Like a door is it!"

"A door?" questioned Lord Red.

"A door," said Lord Green evenly.

"A door!" gulped Lord Yellow nervously.

The hall buzzed with excited conversation.

"Peace! Everyone be still!" cried King Krystal, raising his hands. Scragtail flitted up and perched on his shoulder. All eyes fastened on the king.

"Last night I had a hopeful dream, a dream too good to believe. The heavens opened and a great and fuming engine spewed forth swirling darkness, lightning, gloom and storm! The dim figure of a hero stepped forth to rescue my queen!"

"Y'Majesty, pardons," the gossip said in a cautious tone, "is no engine, this door: no gears, no pulleys, no triggers or reels; no flasks, no tubes, no levers or wheels. Has appeared

through this doorway a stranger! Have him in custody the
mumpokers do!"

"Let us meet our hero!" announced the king.

"What if he's not our hero?" gasped Lord Yellow. "What if
he kidnapped the queen? What if he threatens us?"

The doors to the hall flew open. With many a Ho! and
Watch out!, the crowd of lords and ladies scattered to either
side. The musicians dragged their cumbersome instruments
out of harm's way with a horrible clatter. The marble floor was
strewn with napkins, food scraps, and an orphaned shoe here
and there left behind by one of the panicked people.

In strode the mumpokers bearing their long black lances,
waddling toward the raised throne where the king waited. In
their midst walked the mysterious visitor from the Dream Engine, who yelped "Ouch!" as one of the mumpokers jabbed
him in the rear end with his lance.

"It's a monster!" cried Lord Yellow, covering his mouth.

"A strangely dressed monster," said Lord Green, resting his
delicate opera glasses upon his nose.

Lord Red furrowed his brow. "A monster a full head taller
than myself—no funny comments, Prince!"

The creature was about five feet tall, rather rough in
appearance—but nicely groomed for a monster, with chestnut
curls lying neatly on his shoulders. He studied the people with
intelligent blue eyes, looking them up and down as they were
looking back and studying him. He wore a tight black leather
coat with no arms; the arms had evidently been torn off and
sewn on the outside of his leggings, waving noiselessly as he
walked. Atop his head he wore a black hat with two wings

curled up on either side. His belt was adorned with silver disks, with an even larger silver medallion in front, while a coil of glowing blue rope dangled from the side of his belt and slapped against his thigh. His pointed black boots jingled like bells as he walked.

They halted at the bottom of the stairs. Lord Yellow scampered behind Lord Green, who grew quite perturbed and turned this way and that, trying to shoo him away.

The captain of the mumpokers stomped forward in his large boots and, with a great elaborate flourish, bowed ridiculously low before the king. "Your Majesty!" he said.

"See the fellow standing there
Worn and torn with wear and tear!
We poked 'im here
We poked 'im there!
We poked him in his underwear!

Through a flashing door up there
Strangers, dangers everywhere!
We poked 'im here
We poked 'im there!
We poked 'im in his derriere!"

"Thank you, Captain," said the king, looking at the stranger suspiciously. The mumpokers turned and marched in orderly fashion out of the hall, mumbling and grumbling their poking song.

The king, his silver cane in hand, gingerly picked his way

down to the foot of the stairs. Scragtail fluttered its white, leathery wings at each step.

"Welcome to the kingdom of Elidor!" he said. "I am King Krystal." After a few moments of curious silence, during which the king had expected a response, he peered out from beneath his bushy white eyebrows and added, "And yours?"

"The name's Danny Ray, sir!" exclaimed the creature. His yellow-and-red striped shirtsleeve rose in the air as he touched the rim of his hat. "And I'm the best dang rodeo cowboy in Oklahoma."

⋟ 3 ⋞

Princess Amber

"Where are you from, lad?" asked King Krystal.

"Muskogee, Oklahoma, sir," replied Danny Ray. "Well, not exactly—I'm really from Tahlequah, but most folks don't know where Tahlequah is, so I just say I'm from Muskogee." He pushed his hat back off his forehead. "But I am the best rodeo cowboy in Oklahoma—Junior Division, of course."

"Of course." The king could not hide his astonishment. "Danny Ray, the situation here in Elidor is very serious. Last night, some thieving thieves kidnapped my queen! She must be rescued and returned to me!"

"Just point me in the right direction and I'll head on out!" said the cowboy.

"But, Danny Ray." The king frowned. "Is there anyone else coming to help you . . . help us?"

Scragtail imitated the king's expression and grimaced at the cowboy.

"Shoot! I'm all the hero you need for rescuing your queen, sir!" chuckled Danny Ray.

"Many pardons, young man," said Lord Green, sticking his head forward like a snake, "but what exactly is a rodeo cowboy?"

"Well, you sit yourself down on the back of one of the meanest, stinkiest, ugliest, orneriest bulls you ever saw. You bust out of the pen like gangbusters and ride 'im for six seconds, jump off, and then run for your life!"

"This adventure is not some frolicking, joy-filled six seconds' worth of fun!" scoffed Lord Yellow.

"And look at all that flapping leather!" laughed the prince, pointing at the cowboy's chaps. "You can't be a hero without a big silver sword and a shield!"

A squat, red-faced man with a curling black mustachio stepped forward. "I am Lord Red!" His crimson robes were intricately sewn with hearts and butterflies and studded with diamonds.

"My pleasure." Danny Ray touched the rim of his hat again.

"Well, it won't be your pleasure when you hear what I have to say!" Lord Red, his mustachio slanting sideways in a sneer, took a deep breath. "I'm sure this rodeo-champion thing is a formidable honor, but fearful and treacherous monsters await you outside Elidor!"

"Yes!" said the prince, pointing a sugar-coated finger at the cowboy. "Such as bollhockers that suck out your brains through your nose! There are changelings; devils; muddle-bunks; blubberthroats; dark elves; fays; pucks; skull-mungers; wug-muffins; satyrs; mal-gooligan-hooligans; tinglehoofs; and tittlewhumps!"

Lord Green flicked his tongue and continued: "There are

red throats; coal-trolls; hellwains; black thieves; castleraggs; shokkel-clays; swaithes; padi-foots; fiends; ghouls; trows and kongltrows; centaurs; gargoyles; hobhoulards; boggles; dud-men; and the dreaded Sarksa pirates!"

"Danny Ray," said the king skeptically, "I admire your will-ingness. But I'm afraid this task will be too difficult for you!" King Krystal sighed and leaned on his silver cane and pulled thoughtfully at his milky-white beard. "And yet I must believe that the Lord Advocate sent you!"

"But, Your Majesty, the engine in your dreams cannot be at fault," said Lord Red. "Machines cannot make decisions, even bad ones, right? But maybe the Lord Advocate accidentally pulled a wrong lever, set a wrong gear in motion, and so mis-takenly sent us this rodeo person."

"One moment," said Lord Green, musing on certain advan-tages that might come his way if Danny Ray failed in his quest. "Perhaps this cowboy should lead the rescue after all."

"Ha, ha, ha! I'll bet he gets lost the second he leaves the palace!" cackled the prince, taking another mouthful of pastry.

Danny Ray lifted his chin proudly.

"Back home in Oklahoma no one thought I'd win Goat Ty-ing when I was a peewee, but I did. And no one thought I'd win Bareback when I was only a buckaroo, but I done it. Last year I won Calf Roping and this year I won Oklahoma Junior Champion in Bull Riding: I got a new saddle and this here belt buckle to prove it!" He gestured to the large ornate medallion crowning the front of his belt.

King Krystal smiled to himself. He couldn't help but warm to this courageous cowboy and ushered him by the arm up the stairs to the top of the dais. "I should never doubt the Lord Advocate, Danny Ray. He expressly sent you to us by magical and extraordinary means!"

Danny Ray felt a hand press on his arm, as soft and cool as the water from a sparkling mountain brook. His eyes followed the delicate white hand to a delicate white arm until he found himself staring into a pair of lovely gray eyes sparkling like Carson City silver dollars, set in a creamy white face the color of Louisiana alabaster.

"My daughter, Princess Amber," offered the king.

Danny Ray swept off his hat in the presence of the princess and stroked its black-and-white turkey feather. She was exactly Danny Ray's height and wore a glimmering white dress sewn with an intricate pattern of suns and dragonflies and damselflies, gathered at the waist by a gold chain. Her hair fell like honey-colored gold over her shoulders. A small laced cap of gold and rubies dangled a single emerald upon her forehead.

"Danny Ray," she said, and her voice sounded light and merry, like sunlight dancing on water. "I believe you can rescue the queen!"

Scragtail's ears tensed as it heard a new sound, smelled a new odor. The little dragon called out a warning.

The crowd opened to reveal a dark, squat figure walking from the main doors toward the throne. This intruder, this dark menace from the Southlands, walked to the foot of the stairs. His red eyes glowered up at the dais and came to rest on Princess Amber and the cowboy.

Danny Ray noticed his great horns etched with gold and silver. Upon his chest hung a heavy, dull medallion inscribed with the symbol of Trowland: a wolf eating of the moon. He was robed in red—or was it black?—for the velvety texture of his cloak shifted from one lurid color to another, displaying all the infernal colors. He placed his foot on the bottom stair.

"Stop right there, whoever you are," said Danny Ray, putting on his hat.

The messenger of Dru-Mordeloch wrinkled his brow as he considered the stranger. His short, hairy ears twitched. "Who might you be with so insulting a tongue?"

"I'm Danny Ray, a championship cowboy from Tahlequah, Oklahoma. What's it to you?"

The dark, horned creature said thickly, "I am high councillor of King Dru-Mordeloch of Trowland. He sends a message not to you, but to King Krystal of Elidor and to his lords."

"I stand here for King Krystal!" said Lord Red firmly.

As the dark messenger opened his sharp-toothed mouth, a centipede escaped and scurried down the side of his neck. "Now hath the cycle of seasons come to full strength, when kings go out to war. Now are the armies of King Dru-Mordeloch ready with full might to march on this fair kingdom—to take it by force!"

"We have done Trowland no harm!" King Krystal said.

The high councillor's eyes flashed. "To the contrary! Last year King Dru-Mordeloch, in his majesty and splendor, did offer marriage to your daughter, Princess Amber. He was refused! Insulted! And the world as spectator did laugh at him."

"She is too young," replied King Krystal with pleading in his voice.

"And I do not wish to be queen in dark, faraway Trowland," said the princess, looking the messenger up and down.

"Nevertheless, the insult stands," replied the high councillor. "But let it not be said that King Dru-Mordeloch lacks mercy. Or a sense of sport, ha? King Krystal, you may choose the site of the confrontation—on the field of battle or on the chessboard."

"Why doesn't Dru-Mordeloch just attack with his armies?" whispered Lord Yellow, wringing his hands.

"War will cost him many soldiers," replied King Krystal. "And a great part of Elidor will be broken and burned. No. He prefers a nice ripe plum, unsmashed, unspoiled."

"At least we now know that Dru-Mordeloch is the perpetrator of the queen's disappearance," said Lord Red. "He knows we cannot win the chess game without the queen!"

Danny Ray said softly, "Seems to me, sir, you best play for time."

The king's nostrils flared as he thought for a moment. He addressed the representative of Trowland. "You may tell Dru-Mordeloch I will play him a game of chess for Elidor. But on one condition. The game will be played in two weeks' time."

The high councillor thought in his own turn and said, "Agreed!" Then he set his teeth on edge and pointed a gnarled finger, like an old dry stick, at the king and shouted, "Mark my words! In two weeks King Dru-Mordeloch will sit supreme as king in Elidor—and you, Princess Amber, as his queen! Not even the Lord Advocate can save you from the power of Trowland!"

Danny Ray smelled the scent of decaying flesh as the ambassador turned and left the hall, a large, barbed tail trailing the floor beneath his robe.

"Danny Ray," said the king, "treacherous is the enemy of Elidor! In two weeks I must play the Great Chess Game. If you fail in your quest, or if you're late by even one day, this graceful kingdom and my daughter will be given over to evil King Dru-Mordeloch. And although I am impressed with you, Danny Ray, I cannot allow you to venture forth alone into this frightful world. Lord Red!"

The massive bulldog of a man stepped forward and drew his sword.

"Lord Green!" announced King Krystal.

Lord Green waved his arms, and fiery balls of purple, green, orange, and blue appeared out of nowhere, floating above his head, sputtering and humming as he juggled them higher and higher, tendrils of colored flame falling down and vanishing in a puff of sparks. With a loud crackling POP! the balls exploded into a shower of fireworks to the oohs and aahs of the crowd.

"These two lords shall accompany you, Danny Ray," said King Krystal, giving a sidelong glance at the quivering, cowardly form of Lord Yellow.

"I want to go too!" snapped the prince, hitching his sword belt tighter around his polka-dot robe.

"No, no!" replied King Krystal, placing a gentle hand on his shoulder. "You must stay here in the safety of the palace."

"Nuts on you!" The prince pouted. "I'm tired of being left out!" He wound up and threw what was left of his pastry at Lord Red and Lord Green, but missed badly, hitting Danny

Ray squarely on the arm. His beautiful red-and-yellow shirt-sleeve dripped with purple gore.

Danny Ray stopped smiling. His lips went thin.

"I promise you can go on the next adventure!" offered King Krystal. "It's far too dangerous."

"No! I want to go now!" The crowd gasped as the prince viciously kicked away the king's silver cane. King Krystal fell to one knee, his cane clattering noisily down the marble stairs, and the gossip flitted upward, turning dark brown as it came to rest on the roof's dark arches. The king's crown slipped off his head but did not break, rolling to the feet of an astonished Lord Red. Lord Green smiled inwardly to see the king so disheveled and humiliated.

"Father!" cried Princess Amber, helping the king back to his feet.

Danny Ray clambered down the stairs and retrieved the king's silver cane as Lord Red fixed the crown back on his head. The king looked long and hard at the pugnacious red-head and said, "You are a nasty prince, an ill-tempered prince, a disagreeable and spoiled prince! You will have your way even though it may kill you. I hope this dangerous adventure molds you into the graceful and compassionate man who must some-day sit upon the throne of Elidor. If not, so be it!"

Amber faced the cowboy. Her eyes were sad, even grave. "Here is a piece of paper bearing a portrait of the queen," she said.

"I'll look at it first chance I get, ma'am," Danny Ray said. He folded it up and tucked it down in one of his boots. He took hold of her hand. "Don't worry, dear princess, you ain't gonna have to marry that ol' scraggly King Dru-Mordeloch! I'll see to it!"

"I'm the one who will see to it!" butted in the prince. "I'm in charge of this adventure!"

A tall, glittering figure came to stand at the foot of the stairs. His uniform flashed purple and silver, his chest was adorned with medals, and his captain's hat sparkled in his hand.

"Your Majesty, Captain Shimmersheen at your service!" His long handlebar mustachio tilted from side to side as he wiggled his nose. "My ship, the *Anabella*, is fast! She rides anchor in Birdwhistle Bay but she can sail within the hour!"

"Thank you, Captain!" replied King Krystal, deeply moved at the sudden good fortune. "With such a fine vessel as *Anabella*, we are assured of success. Summon my clerk to draw up a document authorizing Danny Ray to rescue my queen!"

The junior bull-riding champion from Oklahoma walked down the dais stairs, but the prince pushed by him and with a raised nose led the cowboy, Lord Red, and Lord Green out of the hall.

With a wave of her small hand, Princess Amber said, "Good luck, Lord Cowboy!"

"No ma'am," he said, turning around and managing a grin. He touched the rim of his hat: "My name's Danny Ray, and I'm the best dang rodeo cowboy in Oklahoma!"

⇥ 4 ⇤

The Checkered Sea

 The cowboy tipped his hat forward to shade his eyes in the harsh sunlight. A polished plain of black marble, shining like an enameled sea, stretched out in all directions. Soaring clouds, mirrored in the polished stone, rose swiftly over the level horizon and chased along like marshmallow chariots in the wind—a huge sky of white puffy fortresses. Far away in the distance purple mountains barely broke the horizon.

"Shoot! I thought western Oklahoma was flat!" said Danny Ray. "But I ain't never seen anything like this: no grass, mountains, or trees; no rivers, brooks, or streams!"

"What do you expect?" said the prince testily, the wind playing havoc with his red hair. "We're standing on the Checkered Sea!"

"Why do you call this a sea if there ain't no water in it? Back in my world, seas are thousands of miles across, filled with water miles and miles deep!" Danny Ray stretched his arms as wide as they would go.

The prince's mouth opened in shock. "You could drown in that much water!"

"No kidding," snorted the cowboy. He stomped his boot on the hard surface. "Who ever heard of a marble sea?"

The prince huffed as if he were about to explode into a torrent of foul language.

"Look at you now!" said Danny Ray, frowning. "This morning you're all high and mighty when we sailed away from Elidor with King Krystal and the princess and pert near the whole kingdom seeing us off, a-cheerin' and a-wavin'! But now, when the going gets tough—"

"Captain Shimmersheen said we're insane for walking out here!" said the prince. "I ordered you to stay on board the *Anabella* with Lord Red and Lord Green."

"If they want to sit on a ship with a busted engine and watch the clouds go by, that's up to them," Danny Ray informed the prince.

"And so, instead, we stand out here in the open and watch the clouds go by?" asked the prince sarcastically.

"Walk on back to the *Anabella*, then. I ain't gonna stop you!" said Danny Ray irritably. "Me—I got to keep moving!"

"Nuts on you!" The prince pointed at the cowboy. "How dare you tell me what to do!"

"Look, partner," said Danny Ray simply, "I'm driving this train, all right?"

The prince set his teeth together. "We're not partners! I'm the leader! And I'm not going to forget that you disobeyed me!"

Danny Ray felt a slight humming in the ground. He knelt down. His hand and its reflection met on the marble. He could feel the vibration, like what the cowboys of the Great Plains must have felt listening with an ear pressed against the ground for the approach of a buffalo stampede.

The prince felt it too and he cried out, "I told you it was dangerous out here! Just don't stand there—run!"

The prince hitched his sword to the side so that he wouldn't trip over it, and scampered away. Danny Ray shook his head, watching him scampering away, his polka-dot robe billowing and blustering in the gusting wind.

The trembling in the ground increased.

"Holy smokes!" Danny Ray said.

The cowboy took off, running as if his pants were on fire! His boots thudded in rhythm and his blue rope slapped his thigh as he brought up his knees in quick, determined strides.

Something was coming, and fast! The ground began to shake with thunderous rumblings.

Out of the corner of his eye Danny Ray saw an enormous gray spike bearing down on them like a chuffing locomotive. His breath came in short pants, his heart beating in his throat drummthump! drummthump! drummthump! His spurs rang shrilly and the wind whistled in his ears. His world had turned into a crazy concert of racing wind, angry white clouds, and blinding sunlight.

The spike was drawing closer fast! His lungs burned like hot charcoal! He huffed louder and louder—his legs heavy with fatigue—and he put on a burst of speed.

He had almost caught up to the prince when—

H*ROOOOOOOOOOM!*—the wind from something thunder-ing past shoved Danny Ray from behind, sending him sprawl-ing headlong, sliding across the smooth black marble—marble that abruptly turned as white as milk. His hat was sucked off his head and soared high into the air, a small black speck against the clouds. He rolled over on his side just in time to see a tall stone tower vanish over the horizon, cutting a low cloud in half.

Then it was gone.

Danny Ray sat up. "Whew! That was close! That was the biggest dang silo I ever did see!"

"That was no si—whatever you said!" A panting prince dropped into a sprawling heap beside him. "That" (a breath) "was a rook" (another breath); "a castle" (another breath).

Danny Ray stood up and dusted off his pants even though he wasn't dirty—not even the smallest speck of dust. "Shoot! In my world, chess pieces are just a few inches tall—about so high." He displayed his hand with a space between his thumb and forefinger. "My lands! That rook was bigger than a tall building! How does something that big move so fast?"

"This is the Checkered Sea, Sir Cowboy!" said the prince sarcastically.

"It's just cowboy, feller!"

"I told you it's dangerous out here!" The prince sniffed. "Ships sail as fast as they want to!"

Danny Ray's right foot rested on black marble, his left on white. The border between the two squares went off in a line as far as the eye could see. The prince took off a silver slipper and rubbed his foot, his polka-dot robe and red hair glowing bright against the black marble. There came a soft plop! as Danny Ray's cowboy hat dropped down out of the sky, landing right on top of the prince's head! It sat there crookedly, hiding one eye. The cowboy slapped his thigh and laughed.

"We almost got killed just now!" snapped the prince, throwing down the hat angrily. "And all you can do is laugh!"

"No, I can run too!" chuckled Danny Ray as he reached down for his hat. "And pretty fast, at that!" He displayed a red handkerchief, wiped his forehead, and put his hat back on. He looped the thin rawhide strap under his chin to keep it from blowing off again.

"How much farther do we have to go?" the prince grumbled. "As if you even know! Oh, I'm so miserable I could die!" He tugged on the cowboy's pant leg. "Aren't your feet killing you in those boots? Oh, for a good tub to soak my feet in!" he said mournfully.

Suddenly, the prince froze. The ground began humming ominously. His robe turned gray as a shadow crept up and flowed over them like cold ink. He cringed, pointing up over Danny Ray's head. "The rook—it's back!"

The towering rook had silently slid up and now loomed over them. Danny Ray studied its old, deteriorating stone walls spotted with ivy and tiny red flowers, up to the crown far overhead where colorful flags flapped against the blue sky. A group of tiny figures congregated around the rim. Metal flashed in the sunlight. Someone had a telescope: they were being watched.

"Look! A door is opening!" The prince jumped up and began wringing his shoe in a fit of anxiety.

From the base of the tower came a deep rumble, and a jet of steam hissed out from either side of a large iron gate as it yawned open like a black mouth. And from out of the steam a group of rough-looking soldiers emerged, carrying spears and axes, led by a huge black coal-troll with horns that curled around the sides of his face and beneath his chin. His eyes shone with a white light. "This way," he commanded gruffly, brandishing a long pitchfork.

"Now look!" whined the prince. "Just look at the trouble you got us in, Danny Ray!"

❧ 5 ❧

Tantarrabobs

 The cowboy and the prince were led up a flight of stairs into the dark interior of the rook. They came to a stone archway set over a wooden door studded with hammered bands of iron. Over the doorway leered a stone demon with wild eyes and wide nostrils from which smoke wafted up in an eerie dance. Heavy metal bars were drawn back with a rumble, and the door groaned open.

"So, Danny Ray, this is your idea of adventure—getting picked up by this piece of junk!" snapped the prince moodily.

"At least its engines are running," replied the cowboy.

"You like it better here?" sniffled the prince. "Lord Red and Lord Green would laugh if they saw us right now—"

"Quiet!" said one of the guards, and shoved them through the door, which closed ominously behind them.

As Danny Ray's eyes became accustomed to the gloominess, he noticed a huge iron wheel dominating the center of the room, standing on end and turning slowly. The big wheel's supporting timbers were fastened by iron bolts the size of his head. A large open furnace purred softly in one corner, its orange flames throwing dancing shadows across the room. A black silhouette with horns wielded a hammer up and down— clank! clank! clank!—on an iron gear that glowed red-hot in the hot smoky air.

"Over here! Slop chest!" said the guard, nudging over a wooden chest with the handle of his pitchfork. Inside was a mound of smelly rags that turned out to be shirts and pants. "Change yer clothes, lubbers!"

"Slop chest is right!" Danny Ray said, frowning. He picked up a shirt that had some slimy red stuff on the front.

"I'm not going to wear these rags!" said the prince with a haughty tone.

"We better do as he says," Danny Ray said, wiping sweat off his forehead. "That there pitchfork looks awful sharp!"

The prince covered his nose with a lace handkerchief and fell into a fit of sneezing and coughing. Danny Ray's cowboy hat was taken away, but he insisted on keeping his boots. As he changed into the filthy clothes, he noticed the prince standing in his underwear with his arms stretched out.

"What's your problem?" asked the cowboy.

"I don't dress myself," the prince said matter-of-factly. "Pick out the cleanest shirt and trousers and then put them on me."

"Oh brother," Danny Ray said, shaking his head.

"I expect you to button the shirt properly—the first time!"

"Get goin'," growled the guard, tapping the chest impatiently with his pitchfork.

"Prince, I'm gettin' tired of you real quick," muttered the cowboy.

The prince stared straight ahead, his nose in the air as Danny Ray fitted him with a shirt and pants. The prince's silver slippers were comical peeking out from beneath his stained gray-and-black work pants.

"Uh-oh," said the prince.

Out of the gloom swaggered an even larger coal-troll. A patch of black hair atop his head was pulled back so tightly it looked like it hurt. He was dressed in an officer's coat, and Danny Ray noticed he had a wooden leg. The light from his eyes shone like twin moons as he towered over them, appraising them, hands on hips.

"Whatta we got here?" he boomed. "A couple of real dainty ladies, from the looks of you!" He roughly handed each of them a shovel. "Here you go, my lovelies. And welcome aboard *Hog*! Me, I'm Hoodie Crow, yer lovin' master on this here voyage. Keep yer backs to shovelin' coal, don't sass me, and we'll get along jist fine."

"There's been a mistake!" piped the prince. "Me and this cowboy are on a very important quest!"

Hoodie Crow's eyes flashed. His sharp-beaked nose needled toward them. "The mistake is you talkin' back! Someone gets sent to me—they work! Garbage does as it's told."

"We're not garbage!" Danny Ray said, suddenly angry, and threw down his shovel with a clatter. "And I ain't gonna shovel no coal!"

Hoodie Crow smiled, and a throbbing vein branched down the side of his forehead. "Listen here, lubber—write it down if ya gotta, because I'm only sayin' it this once: *Hog*'s a garbage vessel. We picks up anything unauthorized on the sea. You was both found wanderin' on the board with no good reason; that makes you garbage. We have a sayin' on this here ship: Garbage is in the eye of the beholder. Me, Hoodie"—he thumped his chest with his thumb—"I'm the beholder. And you're garbage—so you gets treated like garbage, see? Now, be a good little piece of garbage and pick up yer shovel, then maybe I doesn't feeds you to the red bats, got it?"

WHAAAAANG—GRRRRR! The big wheel turned, making a terrible grinding noise like gnashing bones.

"Now shovel!" warned Hoodie Crow as he strode off into the darkness.

"What an intolerable brute!" commented the prince. He jerked his head up and pointed overhead into the smoky rafters. "Look!"

Something very large swooped low over their heads and flapped its way across to the opposite wall.

"Probably one of those red bats," suggested Danny Ray.

Nearby, a conveyor belt loaded down with coal chugged-squeaked, chugged-squeaked, into the darkness. The cowboy took a step that way.

"Where do you think you're going?" The Prince grabbed him by the shoulder. "Remember what that Hoodie Crow said! Do you want to be supper for the red bats?"

"This here conveyor belt leads somewhere—and I have a mind to find out where. We might be able to escape!"

"Escape to where?" whimpered the prince, but Danny Ray was already walking along the conveyor belt into the gloom. The deep-throated THRUM! THRUM! THRUM! of the big wheel got louder and louder. Here the conveyor belt disappeared into a small metal box only two feet square. He noticed an axle coming out the other side turning a small iron gear, which turned a larger gear, which turned a still larger gear, setting a whole conglomeration of gears into motion. Ultimately, the big wheel, turning ponderously on its great axis, owed its momentum to whatever was inside this box.

"Don't touch that box!" ordered the prince nervously as he came up behind the cowboy, but the cowboy touched it anyway.

"It's cold! What in tarnation can be using up so much coal without putting out any heat?"

"Listen!" said the prince, cupping one of his ears. "I hear singing and—!"

"If you'd shut up I could hear!" said an aggravated Danny Ray.

The cowboy wiped away a film of soot, which revealed a seam—a small door! He guided his hand across its surface until an old encrusted brass knob appeared smack in the center. He gripped it with both hands, gritting his teeth and grunting, but it wouldn't budge. With a fierce growl he tried again, and with an agonizing groan it began to open.

There, in a small iron cage, sat two furry little men pedaling at a furious rate. Their heads were tilted back, mouths wide open beneath the conveyer belt, greedily gulping down coal. The cowboy laughed and they smiled back with pointed teeth.

"Holy smoke!" crowed Danny Ray, snapping his fingers at them. "Would you just look at them little fellers!"

"You won't be snapping those fingers much longer if you get them too close to that cage!" cautioned the prince.

Long, rusty fur partially hid their yellow eyes. They giggled mischievously, nudged each other, and giggled again. Then they began to sing.

"Give me coal in my tummy
It's so yummy, yummy, yummy
Give me coal in my tummy
Be quick!
Give me coal in my tummy
It's so yummy, yummy, yummy
It's so yummy that I'll eat 'til I'm sick!

Without coal in my tummy
I'm so glummy, glummy, glummy
Without coal in my tummy
Oh no!
Without coal in my tummy
I'm so glummy, glummy, glummy
I'm so glummy and I pedal slow!

I have coal in my tummy
I'm so chummy, chummy, chummy
I have coal in my tummy
Hooray!
I have coal in my tummy
I'm so chummy, chummy, chummy
I'm so chummy that I'll pedal all day!"

"What are they?" the prince asked, peering over the cow-boy's shoulder.

"I thought you'd know," said Danny Ray.

BANG! Danny Ray and the prince jumped as a large, black-haired hand slammed the door closed.

"Tantarrabobs!" growled a low voice.

Hoodie Crow's face appeared over the box, his black eye-brows clashing together like thunderclouds. Behind him stood a creature with tiny spiked horns. He gave Danny Ray a par-ticularly evil look.

"I told you ladies to keep your backs to the work!" Hoodie Crow said angrily. "Normally, I'd have GrimmAx here flog you with the cat for not attendin' to your work."

The gargoyle grinned.

"I like cats!" blurted the prince.

Hoodie Crow exploded. "D'ye, now? Well ain't that the sweetest thing! 'Cause I'd like nothin' better than to have you two get real acquainted. GrimmAx, show our little coal shov-eler our favorite kitty!"

GrimmAx flicked out a wicked-looking whip of short ropes with small knots tied along their length. A high-pitched, whining noise, such as a cat might make, escaped the prince's mouth. Danny Ray was thinking that nothing could feel as terrible as being flogged by that cat.

"But it's your lucky day," Hoodie Crow said, motioning to them. "Follow me. Cap'n Quigglewigg—he wants to see you!"

❧ 6 ❧

Captain Quigglewigg

 Danny Ray couldn't believe the immense expanse of *Hog*'s upper deck—a circle over two hundred feet across, shining snowy white under a brilliant sun. A shoulder-high stone wall surrounded the deck with sections missing at regular intervals, looking like the top of a castle wall. From this height, the cowboy could see far out over the Checkered Sea.

Danny Ray and the prince were surrounded by a crowd of sailors, gargoyles and trolls among them, scrutinizing them with lopsided frowns and toothless grins as Captain Quigglewigg paced back and forth in front of them.

As commander of *Hog*, Captain Quigglewigg wore a faded blue captain's coat with crumpled gold trim and tarnished epaulettes, golden downturned brushes adorning each of his shoulders. Tarnished too were his buttons, which were impossible to fasten because of his big belly, which seemed all the bigger as he clasped his pudgy hands behind his back. His half-moon hat sat sideways on his head, and was in tolerably good condition except for a slightly tattered end that had been

y

49

chewed by a bat. A white feather perched atop the captain's hat and pointed lazily toward Danny Ray and the prince anytime he looked their way.

With his short waddling pace and squat head, Captain Quigglewigg seemed a miniature of the rook itself. But what startled Danny Ray most about the captain was his bright orange face and green whiskers.

"This morning we sailed away from Elidor on a bishop called *Anabella*," began Danny Ray.

"You call the captain 'sir' when you speaks to 'im, see?" said GrimmAx, the bosun, still touching his cat.

"Go ahead with your story," said Captain Quigglewigg, his hat feather nodding their way. He stopped at two folded bundles, Danny Ray's and the prince's clothes.

"Well, sir, this morning *Anabella*'s engines sputtered and stopped. So, me and the prince here started walking across the Checkered Sea."

"Wasn't my idea to leave the bishop!" countered the prince. And then he added, "Sir."

Danny Ray cleared his throat. "And we walked, and walked, and walked. Then I felt the ground vibrating—"

"I felt it first!" snapped the prince.

"Whatever." Danny Ray frowned. "It turned out to be your rook, sir. You picked us up and shoved us in the engine room. I reckon that's about the cut of it."

"Well, have you reckoned how utterly unfathomable the Checkered Sea is?" asked the captain. "What was you a-thinking taking a walk out here? Had *Hog* run you over just now, I reckon your queen-searching days would have been mightily curtailed for some time!"

The soft rumbling of laughter from the sailors indicated that Quigglewigg had scored a point.

"I'd be a-thinking you was making up this whole story," said the captain, playing with his green sideburns and studying the cowboy, "if it weren't for this."

The captain retrieved a piece of parchment from Danny Ray's bundle. The white feather swayed back and forth as he read the document, and then the feather leaned toward Danny Ray.

"This charter was found in your clothes and it names you, Danny Ray, as an agent of King Krystal of Elidor, and bears his royal signature and seal." The captain pointed to the seal with a pudgy orange finger. "Everything's authentic. It also mentions the prince, though I daresay," the captain chuckled, "at present you look like Prince Black, oh, ha, ha, ha!"

Danny Ray had to grin, for it had taken only a half-hour in the engine room to coat them both in coal dust.

"Hmmm," reflected Captain Quigglewigg. "Now what was King Krystal a-thinking sending out two boys to accomplish such a difficult task? Seems that a company of mighty heroes might answer better in accomplishing a difficult task! Rescuing Queen Krystal in two weeks will be a real task for a—tell me again what you are?"

"A cowboy, sir," replied Danny Ray cheerfully.

"Really? Well, I know what a cow is, yes I do. And I know a boy when I see one, but when I picture the combination of the

two, I don't envision anything that looks like you, ha, ha, ha!"
The captain grew suddenly serious, and peered out from beneath his bushy green eyebrows. "Hmmm. And you are from a
place called 'Yokeyhona'?"

"Oklahoma. Yes, sir."

"You say 'aye, aye, sir'!" shot GrimmAx. "Only filthy
landlubbers—'lubbericks,' we call you—would say 'yes, sir' on
a ship."

Several of the crew outwardly grinned.

"Now, where, might I ask, is Oklahoma?" said the captain.

The prince said solemnly, "On the other side of a magical
door. Danny Ray is from the Otherworld."

The crew, as one man, took several steps back, as if Danny
Ray had the plague. Perhaps the cowboy might turn them all
into bubble-belching toads!

"The Otherworld?" The captain scratched his neck. "I've
never met anyone from there. You are a magician, then?"

"No, sir. I mean, aye, aye, no, sir. Like I said, I'm a rodeo
cowboy."

A small sharp object made of wood appeared from between
Danny Ray's clenched teeth.

"Stop there!" cried GrimmAx, brandishing the vicious-
looking cat. He closed in on Danny Ray while several nearby
crewmen drew knives and surrounded the hapless strangers!
The youngster from Oklahoma and the prince stood in extreme danger of being flogged! Danny Ray had no idea why
they were so mad, and the tiny wooden dart in his mouth
played nervously back and forth across his teeth with a great
deal of dexterity.

"What's that in yer mouth, lubberick?" demanded Grimm-Ax. "A poison dart, I warrant!"

"Nah, just a toothpick. I snatched one from my shirt pocket just now," Danny Ray said. "Want one?"

"I want your guts on the end o' my knife," snarled the gargoyle. He drew out a sharp blade and brought it up to within inches of Danny Ray's throat. "You and me, we ain't matey-matey, so don't be takin' on airs wid me!"

The captain raised his voice: "GrimmAx, all of you, away with your weapons!"

The bosun slid his dagger into his belt and lowered his twisted features to the cowboy. "You watch yerself wid me, O'world cowboy," he snarled, and then walked away.

"Weigh anchor!" boomed Hoodie Crow, that black-haired coal-troll from the engine room and Captain Quigglewigg's second-in-command. "Lay a course westward!"

A group of sailors gathered around the capstan, a barrel-shaped object with poles sticking out sideways. Clank . . . clank . . . clank. The thick cable holding the anchor began to wrap around the capstan like a giant spool of thread as the sailors pushed on the poles. And as they pushed, they sang this song:

"A rook is a pig and a pig is a hog!
We haul on the ropes and we drink our grog!
We sand the deck and we cast the log!
A rook is a pig and a pig is a hog!

Haul away 'til the end o' day!
Sing away, my hearties!

We've a lass and a glass in every port,
With grog and grub and parties!

Hog is a rook and a rook is a pig!
Come play the pipe and we'll dance a jig!
We'll polish the brass and that thingumajig!
Hog is a rook and a rook is a pig!

So, haul away 'til the end o' day!
Sing away, my hearties!
We've a lass and a glass in every port,
With grog and grub and parties!"

The anchor was now secure, so the captain spoke into a shiny brass mouthpiece rising out of the deck. "All ahead one-third." *Hog* began to vibrate as she gathered speed.

"Ship there!" A loud call came from high overhead where a lookout sat atop a tall flagpole.

Danny Ray shaded his eyes and looked straight up, picking out the tiny figure of the lookout against the blue sky. What a view he must have, to perch alone on top of the world where the eagles soar above the curve of the world!

"Where away?" shouted Quigglewigg.

"Starboard bow, heading southeast!" called the lookout.

Starboard must mean the right-hand side of the ship, thought Danny Ray, for the captain and some of his officers scurried to that side and pointed their telescopes out to sea.

"She's a bishop, sir," the lookout yelled down. "There! She's seen us—heading our way!"

A bishop like the *Anabella*, Danny thought, the chess piece that moves diagonally and sits between the queen and knight on the chessboard.

The cowboy took a telescope and peered through the lens, trying to pick out the stranger. From this height he could clearly see the black-and-white checkered pattern of the sea. There! A black tower appeared on the horizon.

The captain's next order made the signal boy jump. "Hoist our number and ask, What vessel are you?"

The colorful signal flags raced up the flagpole in neat procession, flapping in the breeze.

"She ain't answering, sir," said Hoodie Crow, the big first lieutenant, his fierce eyes flashing, "but her flag hails from New Capablanca."

Danny Ray focused the glass. A red flag jumped into focus, bearing a prowling white lion with seven stars over its head.

Mr. Piper, the short master gunner, whose gray hair was plaited firmly in a pigtail, turned a freckled face from his telescope. "She's the *Vulture*, sir—I'd swear to it. Why, I'd know her top-knob anywhere! I was gunner's mate 'board her back in '29. But she warn't out of no Cappy back then, sir."

"Ship there!" hailed the lookout. "Another bishop, sir, to leeward of the first! They're signaling to each other—heading our way!"

"I don't like this," muttered the captain, gazing through his glass. "Ah! I can see 'em. Look at 'em fly! They're not under bobs like us." Danny Ray guessed that "bobs" was short for tantarrabobs, and that the engines of the bishops were something even faster. Danny Ray again pictured the little tantarrabobs, how they screamed for coal with fiendish delight!

Danny Ray snapped shut the telescope and cast an uneasy glance out to sea.

"What if they're not friendly?" the prince asked, echoing Danny Ray's thoughts.

"Dunno," replied the captain. "Maybe they're on their way to help your disabled *Anabella*." He peered through his telescope again. "What can they want with a garbage vessel like us? *Hog* has no enemies: even thieves and kidnappers prefer a clean board to sail upon." He put his glass down. "For now, you and Danny Ray can stay on deck where I can keep an eye on you. I'll decide later where to put you."

"I'm the prince of Elidor, and you're just a fat old captain!" the prince said angrily, pointing a coal-dusty finger at the captain. "I'm not going back down to that engine room and shovel coal! Furthermore, I demand that you turn this rat trap of a ship around and help us search for *Anabella*!"

GrimmAx was quickly at the captain's shoulder and snarled, his yellow fangs set in a tight grimace.

Danny Ray gave the prince a cold stare and whispered, "Cool down and maybe we can get outta this without being flogged!" The cowboy addressed the captain with an apologetic tone. "I'm sorry for what the prince just said, sir. But you can trust our story, Captain. I'm telling the honest truth— cross my heart."

Captain Quigglewigg frowned. "The Otherworld has such strange expressions—cross my heart, indeed!"

7

The Sarksa Pirates

 "Here she comes!" the lookout called. "Starboard bow!"

VROOOOOOOOOOOOOOM! The first bishop shot by at a fantastic speed on angle to the right, a black blur crossing *Hog*'s wake. Danny Ray caught sight of the red-and-white flag, the lion prancing in the breeze. And just like that, the bishop disappeared over the eastern horizon.

Hoodie Crow followed her with his telescope and read the name over her stern. "She's the *Vulture*, sir!"

"Splendid call, Mr. Piper," said Captain Quigglewigg. The master gunner's freckled face turned red in pleasure mixed with embarrassment and knuckled his forehead. Their telescopes came up again, looking for *Vulture*'s companion.

"Second bishop's slowing, sir," said Hoodie Crow. "She's signalin': *Captain, heave to for questioning.*"

Quigglewigg barked into the brass mouthpiece: "Engine room—all back!"

Hog came to a lurching stop, the bishop approaching them cautiously.

The captain shouted up to the lookout. "Any sign of *Vulture* doubling back?"

"No, sir!"

Vulture had continued on her way, not bothering to circle and support her consort, apparently reasoning that the garbage hauler posed no threat.

"Why have they stopped us?" blurted the prince. "Why don't they just ask their questions with signal flags?"

"Her question might be delicate-like," said Hoodie Crow, standing at the steerage wheel. The black-horned head turned toward him, and the coal-troll shot the prince an annoyed look.

"Meow," crooned GrimmAx threateningly, and fingered the new ticklish cat hanging off his belt.

"Quiet! Both of you!" said the captain, frowning at the prince and GrimmAx. "Be relaxed and take care!"

The black bishop drew closer, humming menacingly with pent-up power. She was taller and slimmer than the squat-shaped *Hog*, so that only *Hog*'s lookout could view her upper deck. Her smooth, ball-like upper structure, silhouetted by the afternoon sky, reminded Danny Ray of the black shininess of a beetle.

There was movement from her top-knob, where a crimson commodore's flag flew.

"Envoy coming out, sir!" called the lookout. From the black bishop's midships a long plank, like an arm, reached out and hooked onto *Hog*'s rim with tight claws.

"Pirates, sir!" shouted the lookout.

"Pirates!" muttered the captain. "Heaven save us!"

Three menacing figures clambered from the bishop along the plank. At that same instant, Danny Ray caught sight of a black-and-white flag rising and flapping in the breeze: the skull and crossbones.

The lookout began to call out again when the first pirate raised a weapon and fired a tiny dart. The lookout let out an agonized cry and leaned over, and his frantic hands let go of the mast. He fell. It seemed to Danny Ray the sailor twirled in the blue sky forever before he hit the deck with a heavy thud.

"Don't touch him!" the captain growled. He reached the fallen sailor and knelt down, gently turning him over on his back. A horrible red wound had been opened in his chest.

"What sort of madness is this—cold-blooded murder!" said the captain, holding the lookout's lifeless hand. The captain's voice sank to a whisper, shaking with emotion. "Stone-cold dead."

It was then that Danny Ray felt a deeper shadow than that cast by the bishop, and a shade of apprehension and fear fell over him. Down onto the deck of *Hog* stepped three tall figures, thin and sinister.

The leader, walking forward to stand before the captain, must have been ten feet tall. Danny Ray was startled at his thinness, like a stick man, topped off with a head fearfully resembling that of a fly or praying mantis. His hide was so black that he shone with a blue tint. His long, thin, whiplike tail ended in a bulbous stinger covered with soft gray hair. The antennae atop his head twitched and quivered, as did those of his two tall officers, who stood to either side of him. The honeycombed eyes scanned the deck, passing over Danny Ray and the crew, and came to rest on the captain. His jagged jaws opened and spoke.

"Stone. Cold. Dead," the Sarksa pirate mimicked dully.

"What do you want?" croaked the captain. "And why did you kill my lookout? We are a peaceful ship! We merely collect garbage from off the Checkered Sea."

The Sarksa pirate cocked his head. A thick, rasping sound, like laughter, issued forth from that ghastly mouth.

"Time. Short."

"Well, then if you're in a flamed hurry, why did you stop my ship in the first place?"

The eyes wrinkled, wrathful. "I. Question."

"Go ahead and ask your question, you—you oversized, murderous, ill-mannered, undernourished bug!" The captain's white-hot anger had won out over his fear. "You have no right to stop my ship—a filthy pirate like yourself, and if my eyes don't cheat me, a Sarksa at that!"

The Sarksa hissed, rubbing together his sharp barbed jaws. A string of greenish saliva dripped from his mouth and congealed on the deck at his clawlike feet.

The head turned, his large, honeycombed eyes taking in the crew. "I. Search. Kowsboy. King's boy." The face lowered closer to the captain's. "Kowsboy?"

Danny Ray's face went hot. With an inner gasp, he realized the pirates were searching for him and the prince!

"What the blazes are you talking about?" roared the captain. "Kowsboy! What a crock of gibberish! You're speaking more garbage than I've picked up in a month!"

"No. Understand."

"You don't understand?" thundered Captain Quigglewigg. "Then maybe you'll understand this!" He snapped his fingers.

Hoodie Crow stood beside a large, stubby cannon, loaded and ready to shoot. Its wheels squealed like a protesting pig as he swiveled it around and pointed the wide muzzle directly at the great Sarksa. He nursed the glowing orange end of a slow match, which he held firmly in his hand, suspended over the cannon's touchhole.

"That cannon is a genuine smasher," commented the captain, "and will blast you into little itty-bitty black bug bits! Now, get off my ship!"

Two sharp spikes rose from the Sarksa's shoulders in a ferocious display of anger, for this particular species of Sarksa, named Sarksa Tang, are able to rip their prey open with these spikes. His two companions grew stern with fury. A soft humming sound emanated from their throats and they beat their tails softly up and down on the deck, thump, thump, thump, their stingers twitching horribly.

Hoodie Crow lowered the slow match closer to the touchhole.

"Time," the Sarksa said at length. "Another."

Captain Quigglewigg looked the Sarksa straight in the face. "You had better hope we never meet another time. On the day we do, be assured, the life and blood of my innocent crewman will be avenged! One last time I command you: Get off my ship!"

With a slobbering, sucking sound, the Sarksa gasped in suppressed fury. He withdrew, along with his two fellows, and Hoodie Crow's cannon remained trained on them. With one last sweeping glance they turned, and in a flurry of the commodore's crimson cape, left the deck.

Once the pirates had passed back within the dark archway of the bishop, the plank rolled up and the door snapped shut. The bishop cruised away, the pirate flag flapping violently in the breeze, the skull above the crossbones mocking them with its death's-head grin.

Hoodie's gun followed her every movement.

Danny Ray read the bishop's name emblazoned in red above her elaborately carved stern: BLACK WIDOW. Then, with a sudden burst of speed, she was gone.

"That was a near thing," exhaled the captain, snapping shut his telescope. "Well, Kowsboy!" The captain smiled a tired, sad smile to Danny Ray. "And where is the king's boy?"

"Here I am," said the prince dully. He was unusually pale as he stepped from behind a large barrel.

"Thanks for not betraying us!" said Danny Ray.

"Betray you?" The captain frowned. "Why, the thought never crossed my mind! As for them discovering you on their own—precious little chance of that! You both look like lower-deck hands—a ton of coal dust on you!"

Captain Quigglewigg walked away, shouting new orders to his crew.

The prince breathed heavily. He steadied himself against the barrel.

"What's wrong?" asked Danny Ray.

"I didn't ask to come on this adventure of yours!" said the prince, his voice shaking with emotion. "You may be having a high time of it, but I'm not!"

"The pirates are long gone," said Danny Ray, studying the prince. "Don't need to worry about them none."

"No, they're not gone," breathed the prince, glancing back. "Now I know who they are. They'll be back. They always come back."

The cowboy hesitated and then said, "You all right? You want me to help you below?"

"Leave me alone!" The prince cast a weary look at the cowboy and then walked away.

"Hmmm," the captain said, turning the way the prince had walked off. "A little nervous, is he?"

"Those pirates upset him pretty bad," replied Danny Ray. "To tell you the truth, they kinda shook me up too."

The captain's features softened. "Don't you have pirates in your world? Sometime, if you like, you can tell me about the Otherworld."

"Back home we have pirates but not anything that looks like that!" said Danny Ray, his blue eyes gazing out over the Checkered Sea. "And I never saw a chess piece with a cannon on it!"

"Well, out here on the open board, it's dangerous—as you well know!" commented the captain. "It's not like being cooped up on a closed chessboard, used only in polite games between rich kings. *Hog* has a few cannons, popguns really, not very effective."

"Captain, sir," said the cowboy, "are we gonna double back and pick up Lord Red and Lord Green?"

"Wouldn't advise it," replied the captain, concern etching his voice. "The pirates are headed that way now. They'll locate your stranded bishop, *Anabella*, and discover you and the prince set off on foot."

"Then they'll put two and two together," said Danny Ray, thinking quickly, "that it was you that rescued me and the prince and played them for a fool."

Quigglewigg's orange features became grim. "Yes, I believe you're right, Danny Ray. Hmmm. The commodore will probably sail back this way and scour the coast as far as Cricket Mill, thinking that we will stay to our original course."

"Do you think we need to sail in a different direction, sir?" asked Danny Ray.

"You're a clever young man," remarked the captain with a smile. "The Sarksa are an unforgiving brood, offspring of perdition, a race of ruthless murderers, known for having burning, long memories. And they hate, absolutely hate, to be tricked. Your quest is not my quest, understand? But whether I like it or not, *Hog* is now on the run. We will sail north for Port Palnacky. I'm afraid the *Anabella* is on her own!"

"Is Port Palnacky close by, sir?"

Captain Quigglewigg scanned the evening sky, visualizing a map of the Checkered Sea. "Oh, a thousand miles north of here. It's much larger than Cricket Mill, so there's better chance of finding your kidnapped queen."

Hoodie Crow, huge, dark, and serious, thudded across the deck with his wooden leg, bellowing orders in a deep, booming voice.

The normal vibration of *Hog* dwindled until the ship came

to a complete stop and sailors scampered here and there in an organized chaos. Captain Quigglewigg spoke into a large brass tube. The massive *Hog* maneuvered one quarter turn and began to gather speed: northward.

A somber group of coal-trolls filed past, carrying the poor dead lookout, limp as a rabbit.

Danny Ray wiped his mouth and lowered his head.

"Never saw a dead man before?" asked the captain. "Like I said, the sea can be a dangerous place!"

GrimmAx followed behind the group and gave the cowboy a filthy look and whispered something to a friend.

"Those gargoyles don't like me much, do they?" asked Danny Ray.

The captain sighed heavily. "Ol' GrimmAx ain't so bad— when he's sober, that is."

"Sorry to have caused you some real trouble, sir," said the cowboy in a quiet voice, licking his dry lips.

The captain's orange features screwed up into wrinkles. "Forgive me, Danny Ray! That coal room has left you filthy and terribly thirsty, eh? My steward will show you to my quarters below. I want you to take a long, hot bath. Change back into your proper clothes. Go find the prince and both of you join me for dinner at six o'clock."

"Yes, sir!" Danny Ray shot him a sheepish grin. "I mean— aye, aye, sir!"

❋ 8 ❋

The Cannon Arlette

 Danny Ray's memories of the journey to Port Palnacky were filled with beautiful blue skies dotted with cotton-white clouds, the constant stream of polished white and black squares flowing rapidly beneath *Hog* as she cruised steadily northward, and, of course, the prince bellyaching.

"I'm sick of this slop!" said the prince in a huff, sitting down beside Danny Ray on the sunny deck. He jabbed a knife at his food and said, "Day after day, cold beef and peas, beef and peas, beef and peas!"

"We're eating the same food as everyone else," answered Danny Ray.

"I don't care about anyone else!" replied the prince. "I hate this adventure! And I hate you!"

"Those pirates really got to you, didn't they?" asked Danny Ray.

"I've made up my mind! When we get to Port Palnacky, I'm hopping on a ship sailing back to Elidor!"

"King Krystal won't like it," cautioned the cowboy.

"Nuts on him!" The prince threw his plate aside. Brown beef juice splattered on the wooden deck and a herd of peas rolled away. "And nuts on you too!"

"Good grief! I hate it when you say that!" said Danny Ray. "Nuts—it don't make any sense!"

"Oh! And what sense does good grief make?" shot back the prince. "Grief isn't good!"

Danny Ray took a deep breath and turned his back, studying his fingernails. It had taken him two baths to finally scrub away the coal dust. He now donned his cowboy hat, his leather vest and red-and-yellow striped shirt with the purple stain on the sleeve, his jeans and chaps, and his blue rope sparkling in the sun.

A shadow fell over them. It was GrimmAx, the bosun.

"You!" said the gargoyle, eyeing the prince and the spilled juice. "On yer hands and knees and lick up that mess, see? My lads sand down this deck every mornin' time, polishin' the brass 'til it gleams, eh?"

Danny Ray stood to face him. "I'm the one who spilled the food."

"Punishment time!" snickered GrimmAx, unfastening the cat from his thorny belt. "You for messin' the deck," he said to the prince, and then to the cowboy, "And you for lyin' about it."

The prince shot to his feet and said hotly, "You forget who I am!"

"Shut up, little tin trumpet! I'm gonna lay this cat crossin' your royal back, unless you got some way o' stoppin' me!"

Danny Ray caught a blur, a flash of silver. GrimmAx froze, the cat dropping from his hand. The prince held the point of his sword against the bosun's throat.

"Does this qualify?" asked the prince, his hard eyes staring up at the hulking gargoyle. The sunlight played blue and yellow across his blade as GrimmAx recovered his wits and backed away to a crowd of quiet, watchful crew members.

Danny Ray picked up the cruel cat, and tossed it overboard.

"I'll get you both back fer that!" said the bosun evilly. "Jest you mark my words!"

A snarl still played across the Prince's lips as he sheathed his sword.

"Where the heck did you learn to handle a sword like that?" asked the amazed cowboy.

"On deck there!" came a shout from the new lookout. "Land ho! Land fine on the starboard bow!"

"Islandum Giganticum," said Hoodie Crow, appearing from below with a huge telescope. "Islands of the Giants."

Danny Ray grabbed a telescope and pointed it eastward. Beneath the billowing white clouds lay a purple hazy mass on the horizon. Giants.

Captain Quigglewigg appeared on deck with a cup of coffee. He no longer wore his blue coat, but, rather, a puffy-sleeved white shirt, untied at the throat, with his green hair waving in the brisk wind. He laid aside his cup and trained a telescope toward the islands.

"We don't want trouble," the captain said to the navigator, who held the great steerage wheel firmly with both hands. "Stay well west of the islands: maintain present course."

"Present course, aye, aye, sir."

From that day on, Captain Quigglewigg stayed more to himself, staring out over the sea with only an occasional comment to Mr. Piper or to First Lieutenant Hoodie Crow. Throughout the voyage, Danny Ray watched him from afar, a fluffy white speck against the front bow of the rook and the blue sky beyond. The cowboy was about to ask the captain how many miles remained to Port Palnacky when a shout from the lookout made him freeze in his tracks.

"Ship! Ship off the stern and closing fast!"

The captain didn't bother looking through his telescope but ran to a brass mouthpiece jutting up out of the deck. "All ahead full! Pour on the coal! Get those tantarrabobs pedaling, d'ye hear me? All ahead full!"

The ungainly *Hog* lurched forward, sputtering and clanking with all the speed she could muster.

"Beat to quarters!" ordered the captain. "Douse the galley fires!" A young boy standing nearby began beating a staccato on his drum. Danny Ray jumped out of the way as sailors swarmed up from the lower decks.

"She's still a ways off, sir," said Mr. Piper as the captain arrived at the back of the rook with Hoodie Crow and Danny Ray.

"She's a pirate, ain't she, sir?" asked Danny Ray.

"That's my guess," replied the captain. "She's faster than us but we may outrun her yet, lined up as we are for straight sailing into Port Palnacky. Mr. Piper, prepare your cannons!"

Danny Ray stepped aside as the large tarpaulins were

thrown off *Hog*'s three brass stern cannons, pointing out from the rear of the rook at the approaching bishop.

"These ol' cannons ain't been fired for years, monstrous inaccurate anyway," said Mr. Piper, eyeing frightened spiders scurrying away from the light.

"Us'll learn 'em a lesson, sir!" grinned a toothless sailor, busily sorting through a pile of rusty cannonballs, picking out the roundest and shiniest for the first firing.

"Hope they ain't eated yet, sir," said another, beaming up at the captain and then taking a spike and levering one of the cannons around toward the black speck on the horizon behind them. "We'm about to give 'em an iron lunch!"

The excitement seemed to have energized the captain. His cheeks turned red over the natural orange of his face, and his eyes sparkled.

"She's *Vulture*, sir," Danny Ray said, focusing his glass.

The captain laughed and said. "Well, Danny Ray, you're getting as good as Mr. Piper at the recognition game, ha, ha!"

"I thought we'd have more time before the pirates came after us, sir," replied the cowboy, wrinkling his forehead. "How did they check out Cricket Mill so fast?"

"The Sarksa commodore is a crafty one," said the captain, his tongue playing across his orange lips as he focused his telescope. "It's my guess that he sailed the *Black Widow* toward Cricket Mill, gambling that we stayed on our original course, but directed *Vulture* to sail north just in case we sailed for Palnacky."

Danny Ray jumped to a loud BOOM! One of the rear cannons had fired. Several of the crewmen followed the path of the shot, arching high and lazy toward *Vulture*. "Short. Well short," one of them muttered.

In response to being fired upon, the pirate flag broke out above *Vulture* and flapped menacingly in the breeze.

Down came the slow matches on the touchholes of the other two cannon, but they merely sputtered and went out.

"Fix these cannon, you scrubs!" barked Mr. Piper, waving over a group of sailors. "Then, haul 'em up to the front rim!"

The captain was strangely calm. "That's the problem with bishops—they can only sail diagonally," he explained. "*Vulture* will have to run away from us at an angle, stop, and then sail back toward us."

"And then what?" the prince asked nervously, appearing at the cowboy's elbow.

"My guess is that she'll try to grapple us with hooks and then board us," the captain said. "GrimmAx! Serve out swords and cutlasses! Prepare all the cannons for action!" Quigglewigg thought for a second and then said, "Hoodie! Listen: Hide a hundred men or so beneath the middle hatches—but don't let the enemy see what we're about, got it?"

The heavy patter of feet sounded over the deck as the crew uncovered other heavy cannons. The captain smiled a grim smile at the cowboy. "Won't be long now."

Danny Ray bit his lip and fingered the bright blue rope at his side. And as he caressed the silky smoothness of it, his shaking hands became calmed. Funny, he had never thought of his rope as a friend before. But then again, he had never had such a rope!

"Land ho!" called the lookout.

"Port Palnacky's straight ahead, just over the horizon!" said the captain. "If old *Hog* can only hold 'em off a little while longer!"

Ahead, and to the right, two jagged towers of rock jutted up from the sea: Morthan Tower and, farther away, Castle Rock. He had heard the captain warning Hoodie Crow about the two wicked guardians of Port Palnacky's entrance. Many a ship had been wrecked on those razor-sharp rocks!

The captain studied *Vulture* through his telescope as she sailed swiftly toward them at a northwesterly angle. He made an O with his mouth and then said, "I'll wager the Sarksa think we're scared out of our wits, that we won't fight. But our black blustering bug buddies are in for a surprise, eh, Prince?"

"Yes, sir," he said, smiling weakly.

"What is it?" asked the cowboy, drawing him aside.

The prince frowned. Danny Ray thought he might explode in another fit of rage. Instead, nervous fingers tapped on the hilt of his sword.

"I have dreams," said the prince, as if in a dream himself. "The same ones, over and over again."

"Nightmares, you mean?" asked Danny Ray.

The prince nodded. "I see flames in the darkness, houses burning. I hear crying, and the crackle of fire. I see legs like thin trees against the bright fires, and the face of an angry strong man. I feel his grip, I see rage in his eyes." The prince felt of his own arm, as if the dream were happening right then. "I see another man's stern face. He has a white beard and a high black crown. He throws his black robe around me, suf-focates me. I can hear hissing, laughter—"

"The Sarksa," whispered Danny Ray.

The prince wiped away the sweat from his upper lip. "I never knew it before. The thin trees—they are the Sarksa's legs!" The prince's strange stare disappeared as he snapped out of the vision. "The Sarksa always return: the dream always returns."

"You're not alone," replied the cowboy. Around the deck, signs of nervousness were displayed from every man jack aboard. The gun captains and their crews joked around, wiping their hands or cracking their knuckles—each man displaying his own particular way of dealing with the coming confrontation.

"Bishop's tacking, sir!" announced Mr. Piper, looking away from his telescope. "She's heading back our way!"

A rumbling came up through the cowboy's boots as he helped shove one of the heavy guns to *Hog*'s front rim. Soon, very soon, *Vulture* would attack here and attempt to cut off *Hog* from sailing into Port Palnacky.

Danny Ray felt a presence at his side and looked down. His leg was touching a cannon, cold gray iron. But this cannon seemed different, for it was much longer and thinner than the others and had no rust. A woman's face had been cast of metal on top of the cannon, the open mouth serving as the touchhole. Wild hair flew back from the fierce face and the eyes were furious—a beautiful piece of work by a forgotten forger.

But even as Danny Ray pondered the face, the eyes glowed faintly red, and the mouth said, "Are you being a friend, or being an enemy?"

Danny Ray went to speak but then his mouth plopped shut.

"An enemy being near?" asked the face.

"A pirate ship is chasing us," answered Danny Ray. "We're trying to sail into Port Palnacky and—"

"You are not being of this world," said the cannon. Danny Ray could feel his face being scrutinized. "You are from far away, yes? What is your name?"

"Danny Ray."

"I am Arlette, being a nine-pound cannon."

"No offense, ma'am. But you gotta weigh more than nine pounds!" said the cowboy unbelievingly.

"Being that I fire a nine-pound cannonball accurate up to one thousand yards," said Arlette. "Being only that I require two and a half pounds of gunpowder for every shot—and not that cheap powder out of the barrel with the green seal on its lid, being that it leaves a bad taste in my mouth!"

"Why aren't you short and squat like the other cannons?" asked Danny Ray, still astonished that he was holding a conversation with a cannon. "They look so darn powerful and you look so, so—"

"Elegant?" smiled Arlette, eyes flashing again. "Short, stubby smashers are for being up close, when you can't miss. I am being for long range, for being shot by a marksman."

"Well!" the captain said, walking up and handing away his telescope. "I see you two have met!"

"Captain Quiggs!" said Arlette pleasantly. "Being how long since we have spoken!"

"I apologize, Arlette," said the captain, "but now I need your assistance—a long-shot long shot, if you take my meaning— just like the good old days. Do you remember?"

"The question being is," responded Arlette, her laughing

coming through the hollow barrel, giving it a woodwind quality, "do you?"

Captain Quigglewigg laughed and affectionately stroked Arlette's smooth metal face.

"Danny Ray," said the captain nodding toward a pile of cannonballs, "choose a good 'un."

Danny Ray knelt down at the pile and heaved out a single cannonball. It was cold, shiny, heavy and black. He hefted it in his hands, feeling its weight and roundness. Mr. Piper poured in a cartridge of gunpowder. It must have been the high-quality stuff, for Arlette smiled. Carefully Danny Ray rolled the cannonball into Arlette's muzzle. The captain continued to pat the nine-pounder gently, speaking to her lovingly, as to an old friend.

"Wind's at eight miles, sir," muttered a sailor.

"Very good," the captain said with a nod. Gently he pushed Arlette forward and levered her muzzle around toward the target, calculating for speed, distance, wind, and range to the target. He peered down the long ornate muzzle at the approaching bishop in the distance. The cowboy studied him closely.

"Will this Danny Ray being the server of fire?" asked Arlette.

"Well certainly!" said Quigglewigg hastily. "Here, Danny Ray, take this slow match. And let me tell you what an honor it is to have Arlette choose you to feed her fire! When I give you the word, Danny Ray, touch the end of that slow match to Arlette's lips—Hoodie, come show Danny what I mean."

"No, sir!" said Danny Ray suddenly. "I can do it myself!"

"Stand to the side of the cannon," instructed Hoodie Crow, thumping up from behind on his wooden leg, "or she'll roll back on top'n you when she fires!"

"We'll only get one shot, Danny Ray," said the captain in a serious tone. "We have to hit *Vulture* hard!"

Arlette's eyes were all attention, eyeing the orange-tipped slow match held firmly in the cowboy's hand, her mouth anticipating the eating of flame.

Once again the captain crouched down, looking down the barrel. Here came *Vulture*, tall and black against a pale blue sky but still a good distance off, still gaining speed.

"Are you ready, Danny Ray?" Quigglewigg asked, worried.

"Yes, sir—aye, aye, sir!" Danny Ray began to lower the slow match.

"Not yet!" cautioned the captain, his hand frozen in midair.

Quigglewigg waited . . . waited . . . waited.

"NOW!"

Danny Ray laid the slow match above Arlette's greedy mouth. Bang! The cannon lurched violently backward, and Danny Ray noticed Arlette's high-pitched bark as opposed to the deeper boom of the heavier cannons. A crowd of telescopes followed the cannonball, a small black dot against the sky, disappearing along a converging line to intercept the *Vulture*. They waited for what seemed like hours.

Vulture lurched to the side. Her top began smoking and she slowed perceptibly. A terrific roar rumbled over the sea, and the sound of splintering wood and crumbling stone.

"We hit her, sir!" shouted Danny Ray, slapping his thigh.

"Prime!" said the captain with a smile. Then he picked the

master gunner out of the crowd of sailors. "Well, Mr. Piper. Looks like we've done for *Vulture*! You'll never recognize her again by her top-knob."

That brought a rumble of grim laughter from among the crew. But none grinned as wide as Arlette, with thick, acrid smoke wafting from her smiling mouth.

✻ 9 ✻

The Attack of *Vulture*

 Danny Ray had been in rodeos long enough to know you never turn your back on a bull. And while the captain and crew of *Hog* celebrated thumping *Vulture* a good one, the ever-vigilant cowboy from Oklahoma kept a wary eye on the Sarksa pirates swarming like angry hornets around the bishop's smoking upper structure.

"Captain!" Danny Ray said, pointing.

The crew's jubilation was cut short as the wounded bishop recovered, gathered way, and came on, very determined.

Captain Quigglewigg hollered down the brass mouthpiece, "All back! Engines stop!" *Hog* would have to stop or *Vulture*, the faster ship by far, would ram her. Castle Rock loomed closely to starboard. He turned and instructed the gun crews: "Prepare your guns!"

There, towering over the deck of the squat and sturdy *Hog*, loomed *Vulture*. Danny Ray saw movement on the crest of the bishop, the thin, black Sarksa crowding on the upper works.

The captain frowned and said, "Looks like we're in for a fight! Prepare to repel boarders!" He leaned down to grab a cutlass (a heavy sword with a wide curved blade), but Danny Ray's hand closed down upon the handle first. Quigglewigg laughed, a youthful, deep-chested laugh.

"Sorry, sir," said Danny Ray, "but I had my eye on this one first!"

Although Danny Ray had never held a cutlass, it felt good in his hand, nice and balanced. "Come and get me," he muttered half to himself, but loud enough for the pale prince to cast him a meaningful glance.

The Sarksa pirates had every intention of doing so.

Whirrr! Whirrr! Whirrr! Heavy ropes shot down from *Vulture*, like black spiderwebs. On the end of each rope a wicked grappling hook, like an eagle's claw, caught hold of *Hog* and held fast. The pirates began crawling nimbly out over the top rim of *Vulture*.

Danny Ray grabbed an axe with his free hand. With a company of frantic crewmen he rushed to the rim, hacking wildly at the ropes made of tough, sticky black strands. Twice the cowboy missed the rope, hitting the stonework, and a shower of stones and dust flew in his face. There! The rope gave way and fell free. But there were too many ropes to cut away!

"Gun crews!" ordered Captain Quigglewigg, raising his sword in the air. "Full elevation! Aim as high as you can! Ready! On my signal!"

The pirates had just begun sliding down the ropes when Captain Quigglewigg slashed downward with his sword.

"Fire!"

Hog rocked as if a huge giant had nudged her as her ten cannons fired at once. Chunks of rock and wood flew high into the air from *Vulture*'s upper structure. Pirates were blown off the side of the bishop, gesticulating and screaming, falling and cracking open like eggs on the black and white marble squares hundreds of feet below.

"Fire as your cannons bear!" the captain barked. Smoke billowed and puffed across the deck as the cannons maintained their fire. Again and again *Hog*'s guns belched flame, lurching back on their wheels as their broadsides wreaked devastation on *Vulture*.

Danny Ray wiped his forehead. Hot work, but easier than he had ever hoped. The Sarksa were not so formidable an enemy after all.

But that thought tripped a signal of danger in the cowboy's head. He instinctively turned around.

"Captain!" called Danny Ray, dropping his axe and pointing frantically behind them! A patch of smoke cleared to reveal a host of Sarksa pirates, like spiders, crawling up over the back rim. *Vulture*'s ropes and grappling hooks had been a diversion, drawing away the Hogs' attention while a company of pirates had scaled the back wall of the rook!

The air rang as the Sarksa drew their swords, hissing and chuckling with sinister laughs. Their bulbous eyes took in the deck, their spidery legs taking long, quick strides as they advanced. Several of the crew threw down their weapons in dismay and ran to the hatches leading below.

"Prepare to attack!" shouted Captain Quigglewigg, his chest puffing up larger as he turned to face the pirates. "Hogs, gather to me! To me!"

"To. Me. To. Me," cackled the tall pirates.

The captain rushed past the cowboy, waving his cutlass. And then, inexplicably, Danny Ray found himself yelling, screaming at the top of his lungs as he and the rest of *Hog*'s crew broke into a run toward the pirates.

Clang! Clang! Steel rasping on steel, sparkling—glittering—dancing—lunging, and a blur of sword strokes—*clang!*

From out of the forest of thin spiny legs, one of the Sarksa pirates broke through the line. His turned his head and spied Danny Ray in his cowboy clothes. The Sarksa grinned evilly and advanced to attack as the cowboy gripped his cutlass in one hand and his magic blue rope in the other. (Strange, he hadn't remembered unfastening it from his belt!)

Whoosh! Whoosh! Whoosh! went the rope above Danny Ray's head as he let it fly! He snapped the lasso taut around the pirate's thin leg and pulled with all his might. With a shriek the pirate fell, and Danny Ray ran forward, driving his blade deep into his body. No time to rest! Here came another pirate, this one taller than the first, a Sarksa Tang with sharp, razor spikes rising up from his shoulders and ankles. His black stinger swayed lethally back and forth behind him.

Swish! Danny Ray ducked beneath his sword stroke and then jumped back as the pirate kicked with his spiked leg. Again and again the Sarksa lunged and kicked, rocking from side to side as he stalked the cowboy. He paused, his antennae twitching, and then he attacked again. Danny Ray was tiring fast, his breath coming in short puffs. He barely parried another stroke and then backed away. He was no swordsman—no way he could match cutlass strokes with this pirate.

Whirl! Out of nowhere came a blur as a stinger, dripping

with white poison, whipped at his head. Danny just had time to raise his hand in defense—luckily, the hand that held the cutlass—and cut the stinger clean off!

The pirate shrieked, trembling from head to foot, and dropped his sword, sagging to one knee. The rodeo cowboy stepped in quickly. With a flash of sparkling steel, he severed the head from the thorax, and it landed with a thud on the deck!

Captain Quigglewigg, weary and splattered with pirate blood, was fighting off a circle of pirates, several of *Hog*'s crew having fallen around him.

Heavy smoke from *Hog*'s continual cannon fire drifted across the deck. And from out of the smoke a huge Sarksa bore down on Danny Ray, pinning him against the wall!

Clang! Danny Ray parried another sword stroke, but his arms were growing heavier. His mind reeled with fatigue. But he was a champion rodeo cowboy, and he'd beat 'em all by himself if he could just—

Whack! A sharp, stabbing pain shot deep into his right shoulder. He had been stung! Danny sprawled forward onto the deck. He rolled over on his back as the Sarksa settled over him. The pirate wore a shiny medallion on a banner draped across a thin body—the captain of the *Vulture*. He lowered his face closer to Danny Ray. As if in a dream, the cowboy considered the honeycombed eyes, the blue tint of the black mantle, the buzzing of his antennae, and his rank, earthy scent. Danny Ray closed his eyes and waited for the searing pain, the final, excruciating stab that would extinguish his life.

But then something awoke in Danny Ray: a hot, obstinate

flame of rage. His hand closed around the handle of his cutlass. Just as the pirate opened his killing jaws, TWACK! the cowboy drove the blade upward. The Sarksa captain made a horrible gurgling sound and an intense buzzing like a dying fly. His shoulders sagged and he fell dead on the deck beside the exhausted cowboy.

Another group of pirates advanced—there were just too many of them!

There came a loud rushing sound, deep and rumbling, and Danny Ray thought it odd that a clear blue sky could thunder so! Hoodie Crow thumped by with a wave of screaming, shrieking sailors! The remaining pirates braced to defend themselves only to be swept away by an angry flood of silver swords.

The cowboy suddenly felt a surge of strength and jumped up, nearly colliding with Mr. Piper waving a cutlass dangerously about his head.

"At 'em! Skewer all them bug-eyed louts!" screamed Piper, his gray pigtail swaying from side to side as he ran away. "Claw and scratch 'til we clean up the lot o' them!"

Danny Ray chuckled through clenched teeth but he couldn't raise his sword. The Hogs cut and slashed, and so determined was their attack that many of the pirates jumped off *Hog*'s back rim only to splatter on the marble sea far below.

Danny Ray's hat almost blew off as a great wind arose. A shrill whining sound filled the air as *Vulture*'s engines engaged, trying to escape *Hog*'s murderous cannon barrage.

"Look out!" someone warned.

Vulture lurched forward, its grappling lines snapping like threads, and took off southeastward like a comet. The bishop swerved as if someone were attempting to steer her. Then came the whining of her engines reversing, trying to avert inevitable doom as Castle Rock loomed up before her.

But doomed she was.

A bright flash and BOOM! *Vulture* collided full force against Castle Rock. Half of her structure vanished in smoke! Was it Danny Ray's imagination or did Castle Rock, that ancient island guarding Port Palnacky, open a jagged mouth and crush the bishop in two? The repercussion of the explosion sent Danny Ray reeling as smoke and debris wafted across *Hog*'s deck.

"Danny Ray!" laughed Captain Quigglewigg, patting the cowboy on the back. "We did it!"

"Yessir!" Danny Ray saluted with his cutlass still in his hand, and felt a jab of pain in his shoulder.

Piper's black smudged face appeared, very concerned. "Danny Ray, we'll have a look at that stinger wound after we drop anchor in the harbor."

The entrance to Port Palnacky was wild with commotion as crowds of ships with crowds of men madly waved and cheered the victorious *Hog*, evidence of how much the Sarksa pirates were hated the world over.

Danny Ray's mouth went dry. His cutlass fell from his limp hand and clattered on the deck. The cheering faces, the red, yellow, and orange flags, and the blue sky all intermingled and exploded into a kaleidoscope of a thousand shiny pieces. His knees went weak and the wooden planks of the deck rushed up and slapped him hard on the cheek. He heard voices—far away, then closer. His head was being raised off the deck and he opened his eyes. Out of the mist appeared curved horns—the black face of Hoodie Crow, his burly head wrapped in a bloody bandage, his white eyes shining down into the cowboy's: "Danny Ray! Danny Ray!" he said gruffly.

The cowboy smiled. Clouds dotted the blue sky, and the form of a tiny blue dragon hovered there—a gossip, much like the one he had seen when he had first arrived in Elidor. It circled overhead, rolling its ruby eyes down at him, and then shot away, its barbed tail as straight as an arrow.

The sky turned dark. Danny Ray felt himself slipping, falling deeper and deeper down a slide into a black pool of nothing, nothing, nothing at all.

❧ 10 ❧

A Most Secret Ship

 An owl hooted. Elidor slept as the moon rose over Birdwhistle Bay.

Two cloaked figures, like black specters, floated across the polished marble floor of the royal docking bay. A single starstone, suspended above the archway leading out into the bay, lent a singular light to that ancient portal.

The two figures entered a private chamber where a man stood between two guards, his hands and feet bound in irons, his normally impeccable mustache drooping down around the corners of his mouth. His gray clothes were not yet stained with the terrible rigors of prison life.

The smaller figure put back her hood, her golden hair radiant in the surrounding gloom of night. The man lowered to one knee, his chains clinking on the stone floor, and kissed her hand, saying, "Princess Amber!"

"Rise, Captain Shimmersheen," she said. She studied the tall, lanky man for a brief second. "I understand the court-martial court found you guilty. Took away your ship, your uniform, your sword."

He nodded.

"So. It's Dumbledown Dungeon for you," said Princess Amber. "Not a pleasant place?"

A pained expression lined his face as he looked down on his prison clothes.

Her cold gray eyes evaluated him. "Captain Shimmersheen—guilty of treason. Guilty of espionage. Guilty of sabotage." She paused. "Guilty of unforgivable negligence, allowing Danny Ray and the Prince Royal of Elidor to journey by foot upon the Checkered Sea."

The former captain of *Anabella* remained silent.

"But I don't believe it for a moment," she said.

The princess motioned with a white hand and the nearby attendants unfastened his chains. He rubbed the life back into his hands, his eyes blinking in astonishment.

"See here," she said simply, opening a large leather bag lying on a table. The princess retrieved a sparkling purple garment and a hat. "Your uniform, yes? And here are your boots."

Shimmersheen licked the corner of his mouth and nodded.

"I am exercising my prerogative as Princess Royal," she said, "and reversing the court's decision. I am giving you back your uniform; your liberty; your dignity!"

"But why, Princess?" he asked. "What will King Krystal—"

"King Krystal is in agreement with the princess!" said the other figure, laying back his hood. It was King Krystal himself, and again Shimmersheen knelt.

The old king reached out and guided him to his feet. "Dark

are these days for Elidor, Shimmersheen, calling for dark plans laid and carried out in the secret dark of night."

"But what about the court, Your Majesty?" he asked.

"Leave them to me," answered the king.

"But, don't you believe there was sabotage? Espionage?"

"Yes, I do," replied the king.

On the table next to the bag lay a dead gossip, its blue tongue drooping out of its mouth. It was the size of an owl, rather large for a gossip, and the king stroked its head.

"This was Scragworm, one of my favorites," said the king. "He was very strong. When I learned *Anabella* was disabled, I sent him looking for Danny Ray and the prince. He happened upon the trail of *Vulture*, a Sarksa pirate bishop, and followed her to Port Palnacky."

"A gossip flew all the way from Elidor to Port Palnacky?" Shimmersheen was amazed.

"And back again!" sniffed the princess, stroking him affectionately in her turn. "And then he died."

The king patted his daughter on the shoulder and said, "At Port Palnacky, Scragworm caught sight of Danny Ray."

"He's alive?" gasped the captain.

"I have very solemn news, I'm afraid," said the king, deeply saddened. "Danny Ray is dead."

"Your Majesty!"

King Krystal nodded. "He was killed in a sea battle, stung to death by the Sarksa. The prince was nowhere to be seen. I fear for his well-being."

A tear formed in Princess Amber's eye and fell down her cheek like a diamond.

A deep frown creased Shimmersheen's forehead: "Was the queen ever sighted, Your Majesty?"

King Krystal shook his head.

Shimmersheen grew solemn. "How can I help, Your Majesty?"

One of the guards opened a large curtain, revealing the breadth of Birdwhistle Bay bathed in starlight. A tall, black queen was docked nearby, reflecting the moonlight.

"She's the *Lady Amethyst*," said the king. "I have armed her with one hundred and forty cannon and have manned her with a seasoned crew. She is now the most powerful ship in the world."

Shimmersheen glanced from the princess to the king, and then out over the bay.

"The princess has restored your personal belongings," said King Krystal. "I am restoring your command. But not to *Anabella*. You shall captain *Lady Amethyst!*"

"Your Majesty!" exclaimed Shimmersheen.

"Be assured I will get to the real cause of what happened to *Anabella*," said the king. "In the meantime, sail for Port Palnacky with all speed."

"Yes, Your Majesty!" he said, but then he became thoughtful. "I would not seem ungrateful, but may I have restored to me the most cherished privilege of all—the leave to kiss your hand, Your Majesty?"

As the captain knelt and kissed his ring, King Krystal said, "Captain Shimmersheen: You are our last hope! Find the prince and the queen!"

A naval officer appeared and gathered the captain's glittering uniform in his arms. Several other officers waited outside the chamber door to escort him to his new command.

"One last matter," said Princess Amber with a stern look. She held out a glimmering object. "Your sword, sir!"

Shimmersheen studied the ornate scabbard as if he were being reacquainted with an old friend, gripping the cold handle. "It brings me much pleasure to receive my sword at your hand, Princess Amber."

"I trust you remember how to use it?" said King Krystal.

The captain smiled. He drew the blade out of its scabbard, the singing steel quieting as he kissed it.

He gave the king a solemn look. "Aye, aye, sir!"

❧ 11 ❧

Gimmion Gott

Danny Ray opened his eyes ever so slightly. The face he saw was his own, a vision, surrounded by twinkling lights and gems. The face faded. The bed upon which he lay was piled with embroidered pillows and enclosed with white curtains splashed with orange by the afternoon sun and waving lazily in the breeze.

A mixture of heavenly spices hung in the air. Breaths of cinnamon and nutmeg with hints of vanilla and chocolate caressed the cowboy's nose like a mother's kiss. Strange music floated upon those spice-laden breezes, flutes mixed with metallic strings accompanied by distant tambourines—pleasant and melodic but utterly strange, utterly foreign.

"You're awake!" Mr. Piper, beaming, his gray hair newly plaited into a pigtail, peeked in the curtains at the foot of the huge bed where Danny's clothes lay in a neatly folded pile, topped off by his blue rope, cowboy hat, and boots. The sight of his cutlass lying there warmed the cowboy's heart.

"I was dreaming of heaven." The cowboy blinked. His mouth felt pasty.

"Was I there?" inquired Piper with raised eyebrows.

"Well, if you have to ask, then you probably weren't," said Danny Ray, wincing as he lifted his head. "Where am I?"

"Port Palnacky, in the palace of the Sultana Sumferi Sar!" replied the master gunner, pulling aside the heavy bed-curtains.

The cowboy whistled. Not even the rich extravagance of King Krystal's court in Elidor could have prepared Danny Ray for the wondrous, glorious, fabulous, illustrious palace of the Sultana Sumferi Sar: the polished black marble floor flashing with veins of gold; the pillars, each chiseled from a single block of white marble, set with fiery rubies, diamonds, and lapis-lazuli; the windows fashioned of such delicate lacework, thin as a spiderweb, that seemingly only the slightest whisper of wind would reduce them to dust; the intricate purple and silver chandeliers hanging from far overhead with silver birds in midflight; the flying buttresses of butter-colored carnelian supporting the massive roof from which strips of sheer tapestries of white, purple, and black waved in the afternoon breeze like long willow branches.

"What the heck's a sultana?" asked the cowboy, rubbing his eyes.

"The Sultana Sumferi Sar is a woman sultan, and she is the queen of Port Palnacky."

"Cowboy up!" muttered Danny Ray as he sat up. But then he gasped. The sharp pain in his right shoulder returned like an unwelcome visitor. His white cotton gown felt sticky as sweat beaded upon his forehead.

He traced his parched lips with a dry tongue. Piper touched a goblet of deliciously cold liquid to the cowboy's lips. As

Danny Ray sipped, he felt frigid refreshment spreading like ice through his belly, his toes, his fingers.

"I'm surprised I ain't dead," panted Danny Ray, wiping his mouth.

"Seems the ol' Sarksa pirates didn't give you a full dose of poison: they wanted to torture you to death—slowly."

Danny Ray caught the smell of something delicious and said, "I'll tell you what! I'm downright hungry! My belly's growlin' like a homeless dog!"

"Oh!" cried Piper, smacking his forehead. "The sultana's doctor made you some grub!" He lifted a bowl of stew from a tray near Danny Ray's pillow and set it on the cowboy's lap. "I dursn't pretend to know what's in it; probably bits and pieces of creepy, horrible things."

Danny Ray swallowed a small spoonful of the thick, brownish liquid, and to his amazement it was absolutely delicious. He began gulping it down like a hungry wolf.

"Well! Danny Ray!" a loud voice boomed as the curtains on the side of the bed were whisked aside. "Welcome back to the land of the living!" Captain Quigglewigg's orange face split into a grin as he tucked his cocked hat under his arm. "How is my favorite lubberick?"

"As good as I deserve, I guess, sir," said the cowboy, smacking his lips.

"Oh! You'll be as shiny as a shoe buckle in no time!" The captain, resplendent in his full dress uniform of blue coat, white breeches, and black boots, wiped his perspiring orange brow with a handkerchief. "Monstrous hot out today, and monstrous inconvenient climbing up to this palace—a thou-

sand stairs or more! Oh, and Hoodie pays his respects—he's
with the ship repairing, making and mending."

The cowboy looked at him around a mouthful of stew.

"You handle a sword pretty well for a landsman!" continued
Quigglewigg. "In fact, all of *Hog*'s crew want to extend their
wishes for your swift recovery!"

The captain pulled the side curtain wider to reveal a huge
open window commanding an impressive vantage point of Port
Palnacky. A fresh, gusty breeze ruffled Danny Ray's messy hair.
Quigglewigg wheeled over a ridiculously ponderous telescope
supported by a brass tripod. He tinkered with the focus and
then swiveled the eyepiece over to the cowboy, who was being
propped up on pillows by Mr. Piper. "Take a peek!"

Danny Ray peered through the telescope. "Wow!"

Hog, clear and crisp in detail, filled Danny Ray's whole vision. She was docked at a pier between a large knight and another rook. Her crew, like disturbed ants, crawled in and out
of every available window, door, and hatch, carrying supplies
and tools. It was obvious *Hog* had taken a beating, *Vulture*'s
cannons having handed out some punishment of her own.

Danny Ray scanned the busy bay, crowded with chess pieces
of every style and power. Pawns ran busily here and there as
messengers and water lighters. A fellow rook hummed past *Hog*
and blinked its lights hello. Knights with serious frowns and a
bishop or two were docked close by. Someone on the rim of
Hog waved his arm as a wooden platform laden with shiny new
cannons began its slow ascent by ropes, wheels, and pulleys.

"Look at those cannons!" whistled Danny Ray, sitting back.

"Big iron forty-two pounders! Thirty of 'em!" Mr. Piper

smiled proudly. "And some thirty-two and eighteen pounders—brand new, forged by Ajay and Helmsley."

"That means they fire a forty-two-pound ball, right?" asked Danny Ray.

"Well, well, well! I'm impressed!" chuckled the captain. He placed his forefinger against his temple. "Most landlubbers are numb in the head—believe a forty-two pounder means the cannon weighs only forty-two pounds!"

Danny grinned inwardly at his private joke. It made him think of Arlette. He hoped that the charmed cannon was undamaged after the battle with the pirates.

"With all those guns," said the captain proudly, "*Hog* is now a sixty-gun rook—very formidable indeed, even with our slow tantarrabobs!"

Danny Ray whistled again. "Next time the pirates come calling, we'll blow them off the board!"

Danny Ray checked the telescope's sighting again. A beautiful white bishop docked nearby *Hog*, and she appeared to have been in a firestorm. Her edges were charred brown and black. Across her stern was fashioned this name: SWAN.

Danny Ray moved the telescope on out to sea. There in the distance rose Castle Rock, jutting up from the black and white squares. Danny Ray fumbled for the focus knob to sharpen the image. A pile of blackened stones and charred timbers leaped sharply into view—the wreck of a ship. What at first seemed like ashes blowing in the wind was, in fact, seagulls, circling, searching the rubble for a suitable nesting place.

"It really happened, then!" Danny Ray said in amazement. "*Vulture*'s destroyed!"

Mr. Piper cleared his throat. "That's right, and Cap'n Quiggs was taken to the Port Authority for honors and a banquet and all o' us as pleased as pease puddin' with ourselves and ol' *Hog*, a garbage vessel what knocks off *Vulture*! The cap'n got given a flashy new sword and *Hog* was give a gift o' them new shiny cannon as you seen being loading on 'er."

The captain displayed the shiny golden blade, the hilt embossed with pearls and rubies. Elegant writing in a flowing script was etched on the blade, expressing the Port Authority's appreciation of *Hog*'s action against *Vulture*.

Danny Ray wrinkled his brow. "Wait a minute! Once the fighting started I remember seeing you and Mr. Piper, here, and Hoodie. But where did the prince get to?"

The captain drummed his fingers on the golden coverlet. "Don't know. But the prince don't matter anymore, does he? I saw the coward inquiring of a ship sailing back to Elidor."

Danny Ray remembered the prince, his sure, unwavering hand pressing his sword point against the bosun's throat. Unexpectedly, the cowboy felt a lump rise in his throat. Could it be that he missed the bratty, obstinate prince?

Quigglewigg brightened up, changing the subject. "Looks somewhat edible, whatever you're eatin'."

Danny Ray poked idly at the stew with his spoon. "Don't know what this meat is," he muttered.

"Why, its cow, boy! Ha, ha, ha!" Quigglewigg laid his head back and brought his large orange hands together in a SLAP! "Did you catch my joke, Danny? Cow—boy? Oh, ha, ha, ha! A quick wit I am, if I do say so myself! Well . . . anyway."

Mr. Piper said gently, "It's for the best that the prince leave, Danny Ray. He wouldn'ta made a hero nohow. We Hogs was only sorry that you missed all the hollering and celebration— you bein' laid up in ordinary as it were—but we been looking in on you the last couple of days, waiting, hoping you'd come 'round."

"Couple of days?" A shocking realization flooded over Danny Ray. King Krystal's deadline of two weeks shot into his head. "How many days have I been sick?"

The captain put up four fingers.

Danny Ray did some fast figurin': He had only five days to find the queen and get her back to Elidor!

"Well." The captain fidgeted, with an outstretched hand. "Now that we've seen you back to yourself, it's time for *Hog* to sail away. Danny Ray, something tells me you'll find your queen and return her to Elidor. I only wish I had a whole crew of men like you! *Hog* wishes you goodbye and good luck!"

"But Captain!" said Danny Ray. "I thought—"

"What, Danny Ray, that we'd help you rescue your queen?" said Quigglewigg. "*Hog*'s seen her better days—she's just an old bag of bolts and bricks—and there's no real fixing her. We were lucky to make Port Palnacky at all. Truth be told," the captain hastened to say, "*Hog* is a tired old ship and I am a tired old captain who had one day of glory returned to him—thank you for that, Danny Ray."

"But Captain, I need to rescue King Krystal's queen!"

"Feel free to rescue, my young sir," Captain Quigglewigg said with a wave of his hand. "But it can't be *Hog* that helps you."

"But *Hog's* being fixed right now!" said Danny Ray crossly. "You gotta help!"

"Do not presume to instruct me, sir, where *Hog* will or will not sail, sir!" Quigglewigg's nostrils steamed like an orange volcano. "You, young man, step completely outside your bounds! I don't know what manners are displayed in your world of Oklahoma, sir, but here it is not customary for upstart children to dictate terms to their elders, much less to a captain of a ship!"

Danny Ray had never seen a sunburned pumpkin, but that is exactly how Quigglewigg appeared, all puffed up and red-angry. The captain would have chewed a toothpick into splinters! He was in need of cooling off and walked over to the open window and gazed out over the harbor with his hands clasped behind him.

Piper spoke to the cowboy in a low tone. "Danny Ray, you seen us Hogs firing broadsides into *Vulture*, and you seen us fight them Sarksa hand-to-hand. We're man-o'-wars men, almost all of us. Quiggs was cap'n over a whole squadron and he lost everything—so he can't take no more chances."

"I been lying here long enough," said Danny Ray, attempting to rise. "I'll rescue her all by myself if I have to!"

Quigglewigg turned from the window, simmering like hot lava.

"I knew you would say that, Danny Ray. You are a headstrong young man, Mr. Championship Cowboy! Oh yes! Hoodie Crow told me about your little misadventure with the tantarrabobs, not minding your own business, violating the laws and obedience structure of my ship! And I took to notice how you wanted to fire Arlette with no instruction even though I ordered Hoodie to help you."

Danny Ray folded his arms. He glared back at the captain and quipped, "So, you're going back to the exciting life of garbage collecting? Sir?"

Mr. Piper saw the rising storm on his captain's face as he strode back to the cowboy's bed. In hot anger Quigglewigg's orange fist slammed down on Danny's tray. The goblet shattered on its stem! The bowl of stew wobbled off the tray and broke into pieces on the polished stone floor!

But then Quigglewigg froze.

At the foot of Danny Ray's bed appeared a giant nearly eight feet tall. He was clothed in only a shiny skirt of gold spanning his huge belly. His massive arms and shiny, bald head showed the faint designs of scales, so that it was difficult for Danny Ray to decide whether he was part fish or part reptile. His skin had a purplish hue, while his enormous eyes, shrewd and discerning, flashed with deep blue and black and white specks, shining like stars. A short sprig of black hair shot out of the top of his head like a fountain.

The giant's glance went from the floor, where the shattered remains of Danny's bowl and goblet lay, up to the officers of *Hog*. He smiled a row of even teeth behind red lips as thick as sausages as he said, "I are Gimmion Gott—the Everlasting! What be all this crashing, smashing, dashing of glasses; be all this smacking, cracking, jimmer-jacking of bowls?"

☀ 12 ☀

The Sultana Sumferi Sar

 "Who the devil might you be?" asked Quigglewigg with a frown, undaunted by the purple giant's sheer bulk.

"I are treasurer for the Sultana Sumferi Sar—Honor! Peace! Prosperity! Dear Daughter of the Falling Star! Blessed Gem! Rich-in-Magic! Beloved Ruler—be our Guide!"

"All of that?" remarked Quigglewigg.

"The Sultana collects articles valuable from across many lands of the world," the giant said. "I lock things wondrous into her storehouse within vaults imperial and guard them against thieves!" The blue, black, and white specks of his eyes twirled around in a sparkling constellation.

Danny Ray asked with curiosity, "How did you get a name like Gimmion Gott?"

"My real name are Yadi-Wazza Zuzulumar," said the giant.

"What a devilish piece of bad luck for you," commented the captain. "But how does that name shorten to Gimmion Gott?"

"It are a nickname," the giant replied, spreading out his huge fleshy hands. "It come from a song that I sing always:

"There be folks that have
And folks that have not
Folks who say gimme
And folks who say got
Folks with nothing
And folks with a lot
Which are I going to be?

There be folks with a palace
Folks with a hut
Folks with their hand out
And folks with it shut
Folks with a pony
And folks with a mutt
But which are I going to be?

You can have too little
But never too much
Look what I have
But don't dare touch!
Or I'll swat your behind
Or other some such
For got and gimmie are backwards, see?
So Gimmion Gott I be!"

The purple giant put his head back and laughed a booming laugh that echoed through the cavernous room.

Just then a loud gong sounded.

In response, Gimmion raised his massive arms toward the

ceiling and called out, "Who commands Port Palnacky? Who be the wealthiest woman in the North?"

"I give up," the captain grumbled, raising his hands as if in imitation of him.

"The Sultana Sumferi Sar—Honor! Peace! Prosperity! She be ruler of this palace! The sultana wishes a celebration with the victorious captain of *Hog*!"

Quigglewigg placed his hands on his hips. "Now, see here, Gimmion Wazzamunda—or whatever your name is—I simply cannot bear one more celebration. I have attended seven banquets in four days, one with the governor, two with the Port Authority, and four others with various captains anchored in the harbor. I am a stuffed bird! Twice I have had my belt lengthened, three times I had to be helped into bed. Mr. Piper and I are returning to *Hog*—"

The captain cut his exit speech short as two muscular servants appeared, each holding a golden pole supporting a shimmering, golden canopy shadowing the minute form of the Sultana Sumferi Sar. Another servant bore a large silver tray holding goblets studded with gems.

"Honor! Peace! Prosperity!" pronounced her servants. Captain Quigglewigg rolled his eyes.

As she drew nearer, Danny Ray studied her. Her light cream garment, called a shimonei, was straight to her delicate shape and embroidered with blood ruby–red, embossed with pearls and diamonds. Small silver slippers winked out from beneath the hem. Her belt consisted of a netted sash of diamonds and rubies, centered with a large amethyst gemstone. Bracelets of gold circled merrily about her wrists, while her cuffs, adorned with loops of gold and diamonds, were fastened to pearl buttons the size of robin's eggs.

A brooch of rubies and diamonds, in the shape of a lion, lay over her heart. Her necklace was simply stated, diamond and amethyst dancing alternately around her throat like the triumphant twins, Castor and Pollux, supporting a large ruby at the hollow of her throat.

Her black hair was gathered in a tight bun with small pins dusted with primrose rubies twinkling happily. Danny Ray lay transfixed, staring into her unblinking brown eyes as large as the world. He had never thought, in his entire life, to see such a beautiful girl. Just as the moon has a bewitching luminosity all its own, so too, the sultana radiated a soft, luminous beauty that totally bewitched Danny Ray.

"The Sultana Sumferi Sar!" announced Gimmion Gott. "Honor! Peace! Prosperity!"

"If he says that one more time," grumbled the captain under his breath, still angry for being delayed in departing, "I'll pick him up, as big as he is, and throw him all the way down the mountain!"

Danny Ray suddenly became embarrassingly aware that lying in bed seemed hardly appropriate in the presence of the Sultana Sumferi Sar! Even the captain, resplendent in his full-dress uniform, seemed ill at ease in her dazzling presence.

"Welcome to our visitors from the sea!" The sultana's voice had a high tone. "Is Gimmion teasing you?" she asked, shooting a knowing frown at the giant.

Gimmion Gott chuckled, a deep, earthy chuckle, and then

introduced the sultana to Danny Ray, to Mr. Piper, and, lastly, to the captain.

"Your servant, madam," said Quigglewigg, bowing while placing a leg forward.

The Sultana glided toward the side of the bed across from the captain and Piper, shimmering like glimmering birch leaves in the wind. The closer she drew to the cowboy, the more beautiful she became. Danny Ray bit nervously at his lower lip. She tilted her head with great dignity and grace, her curious eyes studying Danny Ray and his pile of clothes.

She motioned to an attendant, who served out the goblets, each brimming with a wonderfully refreshing liquid. She then raised her cup and proclaimed, "Captain, I am indebted to *Hog*. Long have our people been harassed by the pirates, our ships waylaid or destroyed, our shipments and goods stolen. Confusion to the Sarksa! And to the enemies of what is proper and right! Hogs, we salute you!"

"Confusion to the Sarksa!" answered the captain and Mr. Piper enthusiastically, and then drained their glasses.

The sultana continued in a pleased voice. "I hate the Sarksa and the Sarksa hate me. I've caused them much consternation for years. That is why you warriors have such a special place in my heart. I will help you as I am able on your quest."

"The cap'n here is heading back home," muttered Danny Ray, "so I need a ship to take me on my search for King Krystal's queen." Quigglewigg avoided the sultana's inquiring glance. "But other than a ship I can't use any help, you being just a girl and all, Your Highness."

"Really?" asked the sultana. After a meaningful pause she said, "May I ask what this queen looks like?"

"She's gotta be pretty old, Your Highness," replied Danny Ray, "bein' how she's King Krystal's wife and all."

Danny Ray's hand shot out to one of his boots. He turned it on end and shook it. Nothing. He tried the other boot but with the same result.

"Looking for this?" The sultana handed the cowboy a small square of folded paper.

Danny Ray unfolded it, and a shock went through him. "Oh, no! This ain't a drawing of a living and breathing queen. It's a huge ship!"

Captain Quigglewigg took the paper. Piper's eyes popped open as he gawked over the captain's shoulder.

"My goodness!" Quigglewigg exclaimed, flicking the paper with his finger. "We've been hoodwinked and tomfooleried!"

Danny Ray wore a flabbergasted look. "So, I'm supposed to be searching after some chess piece?"

"This is not just some chess piece," corrected Captain Quigglewigg. "No, my boy, a queen is the most powerful piece on the Checkered Sea." He studied her dimensions written on the paper. "Why, *Hog* ain't nearly this tall . . . or heavy! Let's see. White queen; age: one hundred years; height: two hundred sixty feet; displacement: twenty-five thousand tons of Mabignonian white marble. Dear me! Sounds like one of my old girlfriends, oh, ha, ha, ha!"

"If you had sailed past her on the way here," commented the sultana, "you would never have recognized her."

"It's my fault," the cowboy sighed. "I shoulda pulled out this piece of paper sooner."

"Danny Ray," said the sultana, enjoying herself amid all the confusion and consternation, "it seems, even though I am just a girl, I have already helped you immeasurably—is this not so?" Her inquiring eyes made the cowboy squirm. "Now I will help you further."

⊱ 13 ⊰

Clabbernappers!

Gimmion Gott, still towering over the foot of Danny Ray's bed, clapped his huge hands and a short, greasy man scuttled to stand by the giant. He scrunched up his monkey face and attempted to smooth out his coarse hair.

"This"—the sultana gestured—"is Mab, one of the dock loaders from the harbor. Please, Mab, tell Danny Ray what you told me."

"I seen your queen, zur, leastwise I think it was her."

Captain Quigglewigg handed him the drawing.

"Yezzur. That would be her, zur."

"What makes you think so?" The cowboy wore a suspicious frown.

"Not many queens around to begin with, zur, but she was all spangly and new—goes by the name *Winter Queen*." Mab wiped his nose with his sleeve. "She come sailin' in a week ago, sly-like, and her cap'n, a big black-bearded fellow, started askin' questions."

"What kind of questions?" asked the cowboy.

"Which they was hobbleberry questions—where do they grow, what's the best place to get 'em." Mab opened his hand. There in his palm lay a dark purple berry about the size of an olive. "Your queen's runnin' zanzoomies fer dynamos, and them as eat hobbleberries like your tantarrabobs as eat coal. The way I figger it, this queen o' yours is short on hobbleberries."

Quigglewigg and Piper both touched wood as Mab mentioned zanzoomies, for the letter "Z" is unlucky to sailors.

"Which direction did she sail?" inquired the captain.

"Well, she headed out to sea, scared-like, headed s'west on the long diagonal toward Ockberry, where hobbleberries do grow."

"Hmmm." Captain Quigglewigg glanced off the ceiling, as he was wont to do when studying the map in his mind. He shook his head. "With that head start, no one can catch her now."

"She won't find no hobbleberries there, nosiree!" said Mab. He scratched his ear like a dog.

"Say again?" Danny Ray said, perplexed.

"Ockberry's been hit by lightning some days back—common knowledge in Palnacky. *Swan* come sailin' in from Ockberry yesterday, all burned up from the firestorm. I was up Doggy Head way gabbin' matey-matey with her signal midshipman, and he says they seen a white queen sailin' south toward Ockberry but she wouldn't answer no signals. Now, this *Winter Queen* will be low on berries, take my word, and she'll head to the only other place where they grow: Buckholly Harbor. With luck, you can sail it in a day or two—get there afore her!"

Danny Ray had a question. "Then why wouldn't *Winter Queen* head there in the first place instead of Ockberry?"

Mab shrugged. "Most likely she's heard tales about

Buckholly—mighty queer country up there." Mab studied the drawing again and handed it back to the cowboy. "Yezzur. *Winter Queen* fits your queen to the letter."

"Thank you, Mab!" said Gimmion Gott, and pressed a gold coin into his hand as the little man shrank back and disappeared.

"Well, Danny Ray, this is the first news you've had of the queen?" inquired the sultana. "Fair sailing follows fair news, is it not so?"

Bling—Blong! Bling—Blong!

Down in the valley, from the direction of Port Palnacky, came the rapid and panicked pealing of bells: Something was terribly wrong! The cowboy aimed the massive telescope toward the open sea and focused it.

"It's *Black Widow!*" Danny Ray gasped.

The captain took a turn at the telescope and muttered, "And there's another bishop sailing off her lee with one, two— no, three pirate rooks stationed near *Vulture's* wreckage. Well, I'll be black-jacked!"

The sultana said solemnly, "No doubt they have blessed us with their presence for revenge: revenge for the brave acts of *Hog!* Port Palnacky is too strong for the Sarksa to attack. But Captain Quigglewigg, may I ask how you plan to leave Port Palnacky with five pirate ships blocking your escape?"

Captain Quigglewigg chuckled and scratched his ear. "Since meeting Danny Ray, my plans are constantly being altered, as if some Master Planner is forcing me down a predestined path. In short, I really have no plan."

"Pardon me," said Danny Ray, "but the problem ain't so much with *Hog's* enemies: it's with her engines."

"That's right!" Piper bowed to the sultana. "Beggin' your pardon, miss, but old *Hog*'s got terrible slow engines—tantarrabobs. They're steady enough, long as you feed 'em coal in plenty. But we can't outrun none o' them pirates!"

"Gimmion," interrupted the sultana, "whatever came of my little golden dynamo engine fur-ball creature things?"

"Clabbernappers!" said the giant, bowing.

"Yes! Let us have a look at them!" said the sultana.

Gimmion Gott clapped his hands and a servant appeared, oddly on cue, with a white cage. Inside, two small creatures with protruding bellies and long, golden fur peeked out through the bars. Purple tufts of hair adorned the tips of their ears, and black stripes ran down their backs. They were neatly groomed and had no vicious claws, in contrast to the tantarrabobs.

"*Hog* sure could use clabbernappers as dynamos!" blustered Piper. Quigglewigg nudged him and he finished, "Your Highness—Honor! Wealth! Good Meals—or whatever."

"Mr. Diaper—" the Sultana began, but then a servant hurriedly whispered into her ear. "Many pardons—I meant Mr. Piper! But clabbernappers are very, very rare, I cannot just *give* them away, as appreciative as I am of what *Hog* and her crew have done! You must have something to trade for them!"

"What kind of thing?" asked the cowboy.

"These kinds of things," said Gimmion Gott.

"The bright sun and moon
But not the stars—
The Sultana Sar
Her pearl sarong—
That is, until you came along!"

"Hmmm," said Danny Ray, rubbing his chin. "The sun and moon but not the stars—means that Her Highness only collects one-of-a-kind things. Right?"

"Well done, Danny Ray cowboy!" The giant raised his eyebrows. "Yes, unique things be what please the sultana most. But I must brush up on my riddle-making if they be so easily guessed!"

"I'll trade you Danny Ray for the clabbernappers!" said the captain. "Believe me, Your Highness, he's so unique that he's one of a kind!" Everyone chuckled with the good humor, including the clabbernappers, who squawked and jumped up and down in their cage. "But might'n you just lend me the clabbernappers?"

Gimmion Gott growled from deep in his giant throat and said:

"He that loaneth, groaneth,
And he that—"

"I simply will not—I cannot—listen to another one of your rhymes!" said Quigglewigg, covering his ears.

The sultana giggled.

"What about this?" Danny Ray reached into his pile of clothes, fishing through his pants pockets, and pulled out a coin. He laid it very reverently in the sultana's open palm.

"Whose image is this?" the sultana asked, studying it.

"A great man in the Otherworld," replied Danny Ray. "His name's George Washington."

Quigglewigg and Mr. Piper craned their neck to catch a glimpse of the coin.

"Is he a rodeo cowboy, like you?" she asked.

Now it was Danny Ray's turn to laugh. "No, ma'am. But he's the greatest President of the United States that ever was. Another great leader who kept our land united and helped free folks from slavery, Abraham Lincoln, well, it takes twenty-five of his coins to equal just one of these."

"Really?" The sultana sounded impressed. "What is this middle layer of brown metal?"

"Copper, ma'am."

"I don't believe my metal smithies have this skill," she said, turning it over and then handing it to Gimmion Gott, who scrutinized it suspiciously.

"No one else in this world has a coin like that one, I guarantee it," said the cowboy.

"A unique coin, indeed!" The sultana paused. "Danny Ray, would you be willing to trade that coin in exchange for the clabbernappers?"

Danny Ray shook his head. "Don't rightly know what I'd do with clabbernappers, ma'am."

"Danny Ray!" blurted Quigglewigg. "I might put 'em in *Hog*!" The captain pictured *Hog* sailing along at over forty knots, snapping his fingers at the pirates.

Danny Ray gave him a blank stare. There was no need to say a word. Finally, the captain threw up his hands and set his head back, letting out a hearty laugh. "All right! All right! You win, Danny Ray. You don't have a chance to fulfill your quest without *Hog*; and *Hog* doesn't stand a chance of escaping Port Palnacky without these clabbernappers!"

"So, you two have struck a bargain!" observed the Sultana

Sumferi Sar. "I'll not ask you to clasp hands on the deal—such a crude formality—but I have your word, Captain Quigglewigg, that you will see Danny Ray through his quest?"

"You have my word, Your Highness," he said with the utmost gravity.

"I have only one other condition in giving you the clabbernappers, Captain." She pulled Quigglewigg aside and whispered in his ear. He frowned and shook his head. She whispered to him again and then he chuckled, scratched his head, and nodded.

In the distance, a long lonely horn call echoed out over Port Palnacky. "The Old Man of the Hill blew his horn just now—d'ye hear it? Do you know what that means? Fog tonight! I must get Hoodie Crow to exchange these clabbernappers for our old tantarrabobs! We must sail tonight!"

Captain Quigglewigg turned to his master gunner and said, "Mr. Piper! Run down to *Hog*. Inform Hoodie to secure only a single anchor and—no! Raise all the anchors! Ropes only. But wait 'til sunset so the pirates can't see what we're about. We'll warp her out tonight, quietly."

To the sultana, Quigglewigg said, "Ah! What a boon! What a piece of good luck for old *Hog*, to sport a pair of clabbernappers! *Hog* will be the fastest vessel on the Checkered Sea! To you, Sultana Sumferi Sar, I not only bid many thanks," and with a sidelong sly look to Gimmion Gott, he added, "but Honor! Peace! Prosperity!"

❈ 14 ❈

A Foggy Departure

The moon hung like a smoky pearl in the fog as *Hog* sat motionless at her docking place, her deck traversed by wraiths in the nighttime—her crew members preparing to get under way. Port Palnacky was asleep, the ships riding easy at anchor like lifeless phantoms. Faraway noises sounded near—laughter from the bathhouses, the tolling of a bell far up in the valley.

Sailing out near the treacherous Castle Rock and Morthan Tower would be a tricky thing on a foggy night like this. The least mishap and morning might find them an unhappy companion of *Vulture*.

Captain Quigglewigg paced anxiously back and forth on the deck. Occasionally he stopped to study the harbor map in preparation for departure, his face appearing grotesque and monsterlike in the red light of the binnacle lantern.

"Ready to cast off, sir!" said a dark shape, appearing out of the gloom, thumping with his wooden leg toward the captain. Hoodie Crow, who had situated the clabbernappers within *Hog*, knuckled his forehead in a salute.

"Very good—but we can't depart yet." The captain glanced up from the map. "Danny Ray is nowhere to be seen. Of all the confounded times to disappear! This is his quest, after all!" Quigglewigg drew close to Hoodie. "The pirates must not be alerted that we're slipping out of the harbor. My evening orders still stand: All crew members are to stand silently at their battle stations—no noise, no commotion. Anyone caught skylarking will get a dozen lashes tomorrow—no exceptions."

"Aye, aye, sir."

An urgent whisper came from the bow of *Hog*. "Ship! Ship, sir!"

Out of the darkness an ominous shape moved toward them. She was a rook, big and squat—a supply vessel—and the fog swirled behind her like the smoke of a cauldron. Clearly, her intent was to close with *Hog*.

"Hold your fire," ordered the captain.

Mr. Piper, who dearly wanted to test his new cannons, acknowledged with a salute and passed the word to his gun crews.

The ship slowed and floated over to within hailing of *Hog*. The mysterious rook stopped, her bow almost touching *Hog*'s. But no call came, as if both ships knew the importance of silence. A plank with hand railings was laid down and three dark figures walked quickly across to *Hog*'s deck. The captain drew his new, glittery sword and approached the newcomers with two monstrous gargoyles behind him, JimmJack and GrumpleJixx.

A slim, lithe figure floated forward and laid back her hood.

"A chilly night, Captain," said the Sultana Sumferi Sar, and allowed him to kiss her delicate hand.

"Your Highness." Quigglewigg bowed.

"Captain, may I introduce some old friends?" she suggested.

Two cloaked figures stood forward and let down their hoods.

"Danny Ray!" The captain scowled. "Where in the blue-deviled blazes have you been?"

The captain's smile faded as he recognized the royal freckled face of the third figure.

"Prince!" Quigglewigg scowled, replacing his sword, as if such an exquisite trophy of honor and bravery should not be subjected to him. "What ails you, sir, besides your normal frights and fears, shrieks and tears? I thought you had run home scared!"

Danny Ray stepped between them. "Captain, sir, I talked it over with the prince," said the cowboy, pulling his cloak closer about himself to ward off the night chill. "Appreciate you giving him another chance."

The prince stood with folded arms, tapping his foot self-consciously.

"Danny Ray, is this your idea or his?" scoffed Captain Quigglewigg. "Where did the prince get the guts to beg reenlistment with this ship's company?"

"Must have borrowed 'em," commented GrumpleJixx with a rough chuckle.

"Trust me, sir," said Danny Ray in defense of a still silent prince.

"No more temper tantrums?" asked the captain. "No more threatening members of my crew with the sword?" Quigglewigg rubbed his chin and considered the prince for a moment. "All right. He can join up again. But, Your Highness," he said, looking at the sultana, "the prince is your responsibility."

"What do you mean by that?" asked Danny.

"The captain gave me permission to accompany you," said the sultana firmly. Two servants appeared behind her, burdened with suitcases and packages.

"Now, wait a darn minute—"

"Yes, Danny Ray, I know," the sultana interrupted, "you don't need help from a girl—or from anyone! But I have helped you a great deal already: You now know you're looking for a chess queen and you have clabbernappers to outrun the pirates. What's more, I brought this—a treasure from my storehouse. Gimmion nearly fainted when I took it!"

From under the folds in her robe the sultana displayed a small crystal orb the size of an egg, fastened to a sturdy base of gold. It pulsated with a faint crimson light. "This is the Heart of Ildirim. It will warn us of the presence of enemies. The inner light is dim, for the pirates are some distance away, but it will intensify the closer we draw to them or they to us. We must heed its red light of warning!"

"It's mighty dangerous out there," protested the cowboy.

"Danny Ray!" she cried. The dew in her hair sparkled, more lovely than gems, as she parted her traveling cloak to reveal a close-fitting leather vest and shirt, leather pants with matching leggings tucked into knee-high traveling boots—quite a

change, to be sure, from her shimmering dress in the palace.
"Oh! I cannot tell you how I love my rough adventure gar-
ments!"

"Your Highness!" fretted Quigglewigg. "It distresses me to
hold a discussion of this nature during the exact hour of our
departure, but you may bring only one suitcase! I will not be
hoodwinked, leveraged, or begged to take aboard all that lug-
gage! This is not a pleasure cruise!"

She waved the servants away and then giggled to see how
flustered Quigglewigg had become. Her giggle was so infec-
tious that she and the cowboy laughed together until the captain ordered them both to stop.

"Captain," Danny Ray said seriously, "the prince and I were
scouting the pirate ships from up in my room in the palace.
Their back lanterns are two red lights on the outside and a
blue light in the middle—that's how they identify each other.
You might want to have the same lights hoisted up for *Hog*—
just in case."

"Very good," mused the captain, quite pleased with the in-
formation. "Hoodie, pass the word. Have our stern lanterns
rigged to show a Bengal red on either corner centered with a
starfire blue. Have them ready to light on my command."

"Aye, aye, sir," said Hoodie Crow, with a disparaging look at
the prince, and then disappeared into the gloom.

"As you know, sir," continued the cowboy, "you're up
against three rooks and two bishops." He counted off his fingers as he went down the list. "The rooks are *Gallovidian* and
Sannox Bay, with sixty guns; *Clackmannon*, with seventy-four.

The bishops are *Wick* and *Black Widow*, both with thirty guns."

"The *Black Widow*," said Quigglewigg darkly. "She's commanded by the Sarksa commodore who killed my lookout."

"Nope. The commodore shifted his pendant to *Clackman-non*, the heavy seventy-four-gun rook," explained Danny Ray.

"Very good," said the captain.

"Pardon, sir," came Hoodie Crow's urgent voice. "We gotta sail while the fog holds!"

"Cast off!" called Quigglewigg. This was the moment the captain had waited for. Obediently, the thick ropes holding *Hog* to the pier were thrown off.

"Start engines."

"Already started, sir," Hoodie said.

"Amazing!" beamed the captain. He was so used to the rough-and-tumble tantarrabobs that the smooth-running clabbernappers took him by surprise.

"Amazing!" he repeated as *Hog* left the pier and sailed smoothly into the foggy harbor. Not a tremor or vibration did she make. "Easy there! Gently wins the day, eh?"

Danny Ray fastened the magic stone near the binnacle lantern.

"All stop," ordered the captain. *Hog* had arrived somewhere near the middle of the harbor. Already, their berthing place had been swallowed up in the gloom. The rook was an island surrounded by fog.

As the words "All ahead one-third" came out of the captain's mouth, he knew he had made a terrible mistake!

VROOOOOOOOOOM! *Hog* lurched forward and shot like a bolt of lightning out of the harbor! In that split second Danny Ray pulled the sultana to himself as they were thrown off their feet, tumbling on top of the prince, the captain, Hoodie Crow, and half the deck's crew in a writhing heap of arms and legs.

No one was steering *Hog*! Suddenly, a shape more solid than the fog materialized ahead. *Hog* whisked past an astonished rook that vanished behind them in the fog. The Heart of Ildirim flashed wildly with a bright crimson light!

Danny Ray raced to the wheel and gripped the spokes while the captain managed to crawl to the brass speaking tube and shouted down to the engine room: "Back to an eighth! D'ye hear me down there? Back to an eighth!"

Hog slowed dramatically.

"I forgot that we don't have those coal-eating tantar-rabobs!" gasped Captain Quigglewigg. "These clabbernappers are so powerful that a third speed amounts to over full speed for *Hog*'s old engines!"

The captain looked about the deck, dazed. How close to the razor-sharp shores of Castle Rock were they?

"Don't worry, sir—I've got the wheel!" exclaimed Danny. He could feel the mighty weight of the rook, feel the slight tremor up through the heavy wooden helm. "You all right?" he asked the sultana as she joined him. She nodded but rubbed her elbow.

"Where's Hoodie?" shouted the captain.

"Hoodie's unconscious!" called the prince, kneeling over the prostrate troll at the back rim.

"Cap'n!" It was Mr. Piper, limping. "Two guns slipped their ringbolts, we're puttin' 'em to rights, sir. 'Fraid we lost Grump-leJixx overboard."

The gargoyle was as good as dead, falling hundreds of feet onto the hard marble surface of the Checkered Sea.

The master gunner confirmed Quigglewigg's worst fear. "Sir! That rook what we passed were *Sannox Bay*! I seen her name!"

"Look!" said the sultana, pointing up into the heavens. A blue rocket exploded overhead, a clear signal from *Sannox Bay* to the other pirates that *Hog* was out of Port Palnacky and was attempting to escape.

"Fire up the stern lights!" ordered the captain, waving frantically. The fog to the rear of *Hog* glowed red and blue. "Our only chance now is to confuse the pirates. We have to pass ourselves off as one of them! There's no going back to Port Palnacky with *Sannox Bay* blocking our way."

"Still heading south, sir," intoned Danny Ray, looking at the compass in the red light of the binnacle.

"Lookout?" called the captain to the solitary figure riding above the level of the mist. "Any sign of the pirates?"

"No, sir!" came the response.

Hoodie Crow groaned as the prince helped him sit up and placed a blanket around his shoulders. Other members of the crew were groggy, groaning as they untangled themselves from the pile.

"Your Highness, I am very relieved to find you unharmed," said the captain. "Prince! Thank you for watching over Hoodie. Conduct him below to sickbay, eh?"

"Castle Rock to larboard!" called the lookout. Larboard was the left-hand side, thought Danny Ray. Starboard meant the other side, the right side. So, that meant that the wicked island with the ghastly mouth was straight ahead to the left.

"You are the helm, Danny Ray," said Quigglewigg, coming to stand next to the cowboy at the wheel, "and you must immediately do what I order! You must not hesitate in the least." He reached out and held on to one of the knobs on the outside of the steerage wheel and said, "If you feel the wheel gripe or tug, *Hog*'s drifted too close to the edge of the square and you'll need to steer her back to center, got it?"

Danny Ray bit his lip. "Aye, aye, sir."

"You sound like a sailor now, ha, ha!" the captain chuckled, and patted the cowboy on the back. "Now, listen. We're going to sail south along the west shore of Castle Rock. Once we're farther south, we'll turn westward and fly as fast as the clabbernappers can take us!"

But the call from the lookout dashed those hopes.

"Ship there! Starboard bow, sir! A bishop—I think it's *Wick*, sir!"

They were surrounded by towering rocks and pirate ships. *Hog* was trapped!

⋟ 15 ⋠

Captured!

 The fog lay heavy, expectant, as if the air itself was listening. Danny Ray could feel the unwieldy hulk of the rook through the spokes as it sailed. His hands had begun to ache, and he found that in his nervousness he had been gripping the steerage wheel with a white-knuckled grip.

The ominous mass of Castle Rock took shape to their left, to larboard. On its shore, frozen grotesquely in its final death posture, lay the broken stern of a destroyed ship with this name fashioned across it: VULTURE.

"Full stop," ordered Quigglewigg into the engine-room tube.

"Ship there!" hailed the lookout, suspended above the blanket of fog. "*Wick's* seen us, sir—she's turning! Heading straight for us—twenty knots!"

The crew members fidgeted, awaiting their orders. Danny Ray tapped his fingers against the wheel's wooden spokes.

"Your Highness." Quigglewigg addressed the sultana. "I would prefer you retire out of danger below deck."

"I'm happy here, thank you, Captain," she said.

Danny Ray felt her warmth as she eased next to him.

"*Wick*'s accelerating, sir!" hollered the lookout. "She's closing with us at thirty knots!"

"Open up gunports!" bellowed the captain. "Run out your guns!"

The deep rumbling of heavy iron sounded across the upper and lower decks as the cannons were rolled forward, poking their muzzles through the open ports, grinning wickedly.

Arlette was being primed by Mr. Piper with gunpowder—the good stuff. The gun crews wiped their hands, standing nervously by their shiny new cannons.

"*Wick*'s twenty squares out!" The lookout's voice was shrill. "She's on a collision course with us!"

The Heart of Ildirim began to flicker wildly with an intense red light. With his free hand Danny Ray looped his chinstrap down—just in case.

"Ten squares!" shouted the lookout.

"Steady," said the captain, as cool and as strong as iron.

"Sir!" the lookout shouted.

The fog parted—yanked back like a gray curtain! With a roar *Wick* appeared, a tall white bishop bearing down on the *Hog*. But then, strangely, her engines slowed. She cruised closer, blinking her lights off and on.

"Why is *Wick* signaling to us, sir?" Danny Ray frowned.

"She's closing her gunports!" exclaimed Mr. Piper.

"It's our red and blue stern lights!" said Danny Ray. "*Wick* thinks that *Hog* is a fellow pirate!"

"Mr. Piper, I'm sure your guns are ready," said Captain Quigglewigg with a cold smile. "Our pirate friends have been thoughtful enough to wait up late for us. It's high time that we put them to bed."

The gun crews chuckled mischievously.

Mr. Piper shot back a grin, then bawled out, "Guns! Aim for her midships, not high up. Cripple her engines or shoot away her steering cables."

"Helm," said the captain evenly, "keep her steady."

"Aye, aye, sir," replied Danny Ray.

Wick had not yet recognized the danger, for she repeated her signal. She was now close enough that Danny Ray could make out the spidery figures on the pirate's upper works. Her beautifully crafted bow, a shield with a coat of arms, was flanked on either side by a statue of a beautiful woman holding a long trumpet gilded in gold.

The cowboy couldn't believe his eyes. One of the statues on the bow disengaged her mouth from her trumpet and stared down on *Hog* with fierce eyes. She blew a loud blast on her horn.

In a sudden panic, one of the Sarksa pirates pointed down, and a shrill whistle sounded, splitting the night air. A shudder vibrated through *Wick* as her engines revved in reverse. But it was far, far too late to retreat.

Quigglewigg raised his sword with the pearl-studded hilt. "As your guns bear—FIRE!"

Hog lifted a little as her broadside of forty-two-pound cannonballs ripped gaping holes in *Wick*. Stone and wood scattered into the air like frightened birds. Danny Ray's ears rang painfully, and the sultana ducked to the deck and covered her head with her arms. Danny Ray had been used to the little popguns that *Hog* had used against *Vulture*. He was not ready for the horrendous staggering BOOM!, and he struggled to keep the wheel steady.

Something hit the deck of *Hog* with a heavy thud—a dead Sarksa pirate blown clean off the deck of *Wick*. Mr. Piper nudged it with his foot.

"Helm alee!" shouted the excited captain.

"Helm-a-what?" wondered Danny Ray. "Well, here goes!" He spun the wheel wildly. While the starboard gun crews worked like devils to reload their cannon, *Hog* turned ponderously, bringing her fully primed and loaded larboard guns to bear on the bewildered *Wick*.

Again the captain brought down his sword. "FIRE!"

The gun crews of *Hog* could hardly miss at point-blank range. *Wick* staggered under the heavy broadside as each cannonball from *Hog* slammed home. Orange and yellow fire raged in *Wick*'s innards, ripped apart by *Hog*'s pitiless fire. The helpless bishop began to drift, not returning a single shot.

A wave of cheering rolled over *Hog*. The lowly garbage ship had been transformed by the clabbernappers and cannons into a ship of war! The crew slapped each other on the back. Danny Ray left the helm as he and Mr. Piper playfully shoved the sultana back and forth between them.

"Silence!" shouted Captain Quigglewigg.

"Let's finish her off, Cap'n!" blurted a sailor. "We'll done for her!"

"She is finished!" Quigglewigg snapped. "She can't hope to follow us! Silence in the ship!" The crew hung their heads. Danny Ray crept guiltily back to the steerage wheel.

"There are still three rooks and a bishop on the loose—and they want our heads!" explained Quigglewigg. "They could appear at any time and deal us the same devastating fire we just dished out to *Wick*. We won't be safe until we escape into the open sea. Everyone back to your stations!"

Back over *Hog*'s stern, *Wick* was silent, lifeless, her crown and upper works tilting over grotesquely. The exquisitely carved figures with their trumpets had been blasted away from the mutilated bow of the bishop. The flickering flames licking about her midsection reflected grimly on the polished squares as she wandered aimlessly toward Castle Rock to join her beleaguered sister, *Vulture*.

"Bring her a little to larboard, Danny, I want to hug Castle Rock about six squares out."

"Six squares, aye, aye, sir!"

Six squares were exactly the length of vision in this thick pea soup, though the lookout could see farther by far. Danny Ray spun the spoked wheel. Castle Rock loomed up before them. Quigglewigg nodded. Danny Ray had learned the feel of *Hog* and turned the wheel like an expert, bringing the rook back around on its original course, heading south.

"All ahead an eighth!" ordered the captain.

For now, the fog was *Hog*'s best friend, that and silence— and the clabbernappers would aid her there.

"Land straight ahead!" cried the lookout.

Morthan Tower's sharp, pointed spire soared into the air on

their right. The old rook groped her way forward, virtually blind, through the narrow channel, hemmed in on both sides by sheer cliffs of razor-sharp rocks.

"Steer handsomely, Danny," cautioned the captain.

"Aye, aye, sir!"

"Danny Ray!" whispered the sultana. Her eyes were wide, transfixed on the Heart of Ildirim: its red light had begun to wave and dance, warning of the presence of an enemy ship close by.

Quigglewigg joined them at the binnacle. The fog revealed nothing. The captain hollered up to the lookout, "Any sign of pirates?"

"All clear out to sea, sir!"

Danny Ray steered intently. The light from the magical stone was becoming brighter—but how?

"Are you sure?" called the captain.

"Aye, Captain! No sign of a ship nowheres!"

Hog was hugging the coast of Morthan Tower so closely that almost nothing could fit between them and the land: almost nothing.

"There!" screamed the sultana, pointing toward Morthan Tower.

"Up against the very shore of Morthan Tower!" exclaimed the captain. "No ship should be there! No ship could be there!"

Out of the dense haze sailed *Clackmannon*, heaviest of the pirate rooks. She was already closing with *Hog*, not in the least fooled by *Hog*'s stern lights. Her seventy-four gunports were wide open, and her crew of pirates were ready. After all, she flew the commodore's pendant.

Captain Quigglewigg raised his sword, but that is as far as he got.

Chaos!

Hog lurched horribly as she took *Clackmannon*'s well-aimed broadside. A huge cannonball roared closely over the cowboy's head like an angry meteor. He flinched as half the steerage wheel exploded into splinters and a searing pain shot through his arm from a flying splinter of wood. A gargoyle's head rolled to a stop at his feet.

Hog lurched violently again, firing her own cannons at the pirate. *Clackmannon* was so close that Danny Ray could see the tall Sarksa crowding her front rim as it came to rest against *Hog*'s rim, rock against rock, with an agonizing, grinding sound.

"Pikes and cutlasses!" thundered Captain Quigglewigg to those sailors still left alive to hear him. "Repel boarders!"

"Repel boarders!" Danny Ray heard himself yell. His voice sounded as if it came from a great distance away, as if it belonged to someone else. He was nearly deaf from the cannon fire now raging all around him. Another cannonball hummed close by, the heat from it making him stagger.

The old *Hog* was taking a beating. Her masonry flew off in huge chunks under the terrible cannon fire of her tormentor. The smoke from the gunpowder had added to the natural fog to form an almost impenetrable blanket of gray.

Then, mysteriously, the roaring blasts from the cannons stopped.

A cold shock went though Danny Ray. Where was the sultana? Through the smoke and devastation on deck, the cowboy ran straight for where he had last seen her, where *Hog's* rim had touched against *Clackmannon's*. Like an old nightmare stored in the deep recesses of his memory came the hissing and gurgling of the Sarksa pirates.

They had stepped down onto the deck of *Hog* with determined strides; with a determined purpose. Danny Ray saw the veiled, smoky form of their thin legs. He reached down to grab an axe lying on the deck.

WHAM! Danny Ray felt a crushing pain in the back of his head. His hat flew off. A mist heavier than that on deck closed around him. His head spun as he lay on the hard deck. He felt along his belt. Where was his rope?

Through half-lidded eyes he viewed the deck of *Hog*: it was in shambles. Wooden barrels had been reduced to piles of splinters; the steerage wheel had completely disappeared—only the stump remained. And Mr. Piper was down.

Danny Ray felt something soft—the sultana's cloak! He heard her scream drowned out by the thin laughter of the pirates.

"No!" he grunted, trying to get to his feet.

Something gripped him like iron around the neck and legs. He was being lifted and carried. And then darkness closed in, deep darkness with no hope of light.

✤ 16 ✤

The Potter Wasp

 Danny Ray awoke with a start and sat bolt upright.

A stab of pain shot through the back of his
head, forcing him to recall the crushing impact before he had
blacked out.

He sat in a large, dimly lit circular room, the walls hard and
brown like baked clay. The floor was warm against his legs, made
of the same material as the walls, giving off a smell like rich,
black dirt. In the middle of the room was a boulder, shiny black.

Danny Ray scooted back until his shoulders rested against
the curved wall. He cocked his head and listened. A distant
buzzing vibrated through the walls. The sound rose and lowered ever so slightly, then returned to its original, monotonous
level.

"UMMMMMM . . ." said a bundle lying next to him. A
face appeared out of the brown cloth.

"Your Highness!" said Danny Ray. She moaned again as he
helped her sit up.

"Where are we?" she asked, shaking her head. Danny Ray stood up and helped her to her feet.

"I'm thinking the Sarksa have us in some kind of prison," said Danny Ray. "Don't know how they got us in here, though. There ain't no windows or no doors!"

Danny Ray ran a fingernail down the hard surface of the wall—no way to dig through this stuff. Overhead spanned a large opening where a ceiling should be, revealing the soaring walls of a larger cave with a honeycomb pattern. It was as if they were sitting on the bottom of a clay fishbowl.

"There's someone up there!" said the sultana groggily, hugging his arm. Insect creatures congregated around the rim, looking down at him.

"Sure enough. It's those pesky pirates!" Danny Ray's hand shot to his belt. "Dang it! My rope's gone!"

"Kowsboy!" came a familiar voice. "Ssssultana!"

The Sarksa commodore was not difficult to pick out, being taller than his fellows and wearing his crimson cape.

"Well, looky there!" muttered Danny Ray, spotting a familiar figure next to the commodore. "If it ain't the high councillor of Trowland."

"Who is that?" the sultana asked.

"King Dru-Mordeloch's main bully," said Danny Ray. "That means the Sarksa and King Dru-Mordeloch are in this together."

"You. Search. Queen?" asked the commodore.

Danny Ray frowned. What the heck was that overgrown potato bug yakkin' about? Sure he was looking for the queen, everyone knew that.

"Queen?" repeated the commodore.

"Queen? Queen? Queen?" cackled the other Sarksa evilly.

"Your . . . best was not good enough after all, little cow-boy!" stormed Dru-Mordeloch's dark messenger, smiling with triumphant hatred.

"Just give me a sword, Mr. High Councillor!" shouted the cowboy. "Or you, Mr. Bug-Ugly Commodore, and get your-self down here and fight me face-to-face!"

"Queen!" thundered the commodore one last time. He hissed a laugh and pointed down to the polished boulder, faintly vibrating. It grew louder and louder. The Sarksa around the rim began to clamor and chant, their stingers thumping up and down in a frenzy.

"I don't like this!" cried the sultana with panicked eyes.

"Wait a darn minute: that ain't no rock," Danny Ray said with a terrible realization. "It's an egg!"

"It's hatching!" said the sultana breathlessly.

Danny Ray's eyes widened and his stomach went into a knot. He kicked his spurs frantically against the wall, but the clay was hard as rock. The Sarksa were enjoying watching them squirm.

The egg cracked and splintered open. A great hump began to emerge, possessing a black, shiny mantle. Honeycombed eyes, still sightless, were licked by a metallic tongue. Damp, quivering limbs unfolded to support a huge, slimy abdomen with wet wings pasted to its side.

"Queen!" thundered the commodore.

"Danny!" gasped the sultana.

"Holy cow," he muttered. "That's a queen Sarksa!"

The queen had unfolded from her hunched-over posture, like an old woman. Her antennae lifted off her head, still connected by glittering strands. A deep gurgling issued from her throat. Bubbles formed at the front of her sharp, meat-tearing teeth: Her Infernal Majesty was born!

"What are we going to do now?" the sultana asked, hugging Danny Ray's arm tighter.

The queen's eyes were now licked clean and she took in her nursery. She was much larger and more formidable than any Sarksa soldier or drone. She exercised her silver jaws, which were laden with sharp, new teeth: teeth yet to feel the tearing of soft flesh, a mouth yet to drink fresh red blood.

The queen drew closer to them. The cowboy pulled the sultana to one side, but the queen followed their movements. Her young eyes tried to focus on what her twitching antennae insisted was right in front of her: food.

Closer she stalked. Danny Ray and the sultana had no weapons, no escape. The Sarksa watching from above could sense that the kill was near. Their chanting rose to a feverish pitch, and the clay walls vibrated with their frenzy.

Suddenly the entire urn shook violently as a large square stone fell through the opening from above, grazing the queen's abdomen. She spun around and investigated this new intruder, lowering her head, brushing her antennae against the hard surface of the rock.

The room rocked again. Dru-Mordeloch's high councillor fell from the urn's rim and landed near the queen! The old trow growled feebly at Her Gruesome Majesty, holding up his staff against the loathsome monarch as she settled over him. The pirates shrieked and fled the rim.

"ARRRRRRRRRRGH!" shouted the high councillor as the queen, with a lightning-like jab, seized him and fastened her sharp jaws about his horned head. He hit her again and again with his staff until—CRUNCH! She bit off his head and swallowed. CRUNCH! The voraciously hungry jaws devoured the body piecemeal. Down that ghastly throat the councillor's legs and feet disappeared. The queen raised her chin to allow the jumbled mass to slide down, and proceeded to clean her claws with her silver tongue.

BOOM! Something large crashed through the urn's wall, leaving a jagged hole, and thudded heavily against the far wall.

"A cannonball!" cried the sultana. "What are we going to do now?"

"That hole—it's our only chance!" said Danny Ray under his breath. "It just might just be large enough for us to squeeze through!"

They began to work their way quietly, cautiously around to the hole, eyeing the queen closely. The Sarksa queen was sensitive not only to sound but to movement as well. As the gratifying feeling of the pirate twitching in her stomach ebbed, the queen raised her head. She felt the sneaky vibration of other morsels in her urn, the strange-smelling delicate creatures creeping along the wall.

"Here is the hole!" Danny Ray said to the sultana. "Up you go!" He hoisted her bodily into the hole.

"She's seen us!" cried the sultana, looking back. The queen

swiveled to face their pale, diminutive forms. Her antennae twitched, her honeycombed eyes locking on to them. Her awful, cold-blooded grin swayed back and forth above a crimson-streaked thorax.

The Sarksa queen's tail rose up over her head, the stinger pulsating with fresh poison.

"Go on, now!" shouted Danny Ray. When the sultana's boots had disappeared through the hole, he took a quick look back and grabbed either edge of the hole and jumped up, kicking his boots against the wall, making a hollow thudding sound.

The cowboy had struggled halfway through the hole when cold wind hit him in the face. He gasped as he realized he was emerging from a hole in the side of *Clackmannon*!

"Danny!" called the sultana. There she stood in the darkness, shivering on a small ledge a hundred fifty feet above the Checkered Sea.

"Hang on!" yelled the cowboy. A loose rock fell from the hole, disappearing down the sheer side of ship. Shoot! He was higher up than the top car on a Ferris wheel!

Something sharp snagged the heel of his boot—the queen was about to grab him! It was now or never! He swung all the way out of the hole and lunged with a desperate hand, gripping the ledge and hanging on for dear life.

"Dang it! That queen stole one of my boots!" The cowboy pulled himself up and hugged the side of the rock wall. "Won't make much of a snack for that ol' Sarksa queen!"

"Don't look down!" the sultana warned, her frightened eyes just inches from his. He could smell her perfume, like spiced apples.

"Too late!" panted the cowboy. The rock ledge felt cold through his sock, which stood out brilliantly white against the gloom.

"What are we going to do now?" she asked.

"Gosh—you sure ask that a lot!" Danny Ray said in a strangely calm voice, and then he started to laugh in spite of himself. Doggone girls!

BOOM! BOOM! BOOM! The sound of cannon fire.

Clackmannon was stationary, but she was turning in place.

"It's *Hog*!" cried the sultana, motioning with her head.

The battered old rook came into view—blessed *Hog*! Now Danny Ray understood what was turning *Clackmannon*. Quigglewigg had embedded his rook's spiked rim snugly into the pirate ship's rim, rotating her on her axis like a pig on an upright spit. *Hog* pounded *Clackmannon* with broadside after broadside as each column of *Hog*'s primed and loaded guns came to bear.

CHOMP! CHOMP! CHOMP!

The sultana screamed. The hideous face of the Sarksa queen appeared through the hole—she was chewing her way through the wall!

WHACK! Something hit Danny Ray's arm—something shiny and blue. His rope!

The prince waved down at them from *Hog*'s deck and called, "Danny Ray! Your Highness!" He secured the other end of the magic rope.

But then the Sarksa queen heaved herself out onto the wall, her huge form looming right next to the cowboy. Danny Ray and the sultana froze, not daring even to whisper.

The sun's rays lit up the eastern horizon, the late stars fleeing to the western sky. The queen paused, sensing the strange
new phenomenon called wind, seeing sunlight for the first
time, cocking her rogue head to view pink clouds in the morning sky.

Danny Ray gripped the rope with one hand. He nodded to
the sultana. She reached over and wrapped her arms around
the cowboy's neck. He hugged her slim waist close with his
free arm, and a strand of her black hair blew across his cheek.

"Hang on!" he whispered.

They fell away from the ledge, together.

The wind hummed through the rope of thrillium as they
swung dangerously toward *Hog*, her cannons continuing to
blaze away at *Clackmannon*. Danny Ray hit *Hog*'s wall a glancing blow with his booted foot and the rope began to draw
them up toward *Hog*'s rim.

"Danny Ray!" the prince called down with a worried face.
"Hurry up!"

"Hurry up for what?" laughed the sultana, the rope having
drawn them just below *Hog*'s rim. "We're safe now—oh!"

Danny Ray lunged sideways as the huge wasplike form of
the Sarksa queen settled on the wall next to him. Her newly
dried wings buzzed violently. She turned her visage of death
toward them. Behind the queen, the rims of the rooks continued to grind against each other, drawing them in.

"Ah!" cried Danny Ray as the queen lashed out with a black
claw and gripped him cruelly on the wrist, pulling his arm
from the sultana's waist. He struggled, trying to wrench free

while the sultana hung about his neck, one foot resting shakily against *Hog*'s rough wall.

His shoulder began to ache, a sharp reminder of his last encounter with the Sarksa pirates. The cowboy panted heavily. His strength was nearly gone. Another violent explosion! Danny Ray nearly lost his grip on the rope as *Hog* fired another unanswered broadside into the devastated *Clackmannon*.

"Captain!" gasped the sultana. Quigglewigg's orange face peered down from *Hog*'s rim. "You must help us!"

The muffled, ominous grinding of the rims grew louder. Danny Ray flinched as one of *Hog*'s cannons was run out, its elegant muzzle barely missing his head.

The queen inched over, her long, thin legs tentatively pressing against *Hog*'s stonework. She lunged at them with her hungry jaws but missed.

They passed into the deep shadow of the crevice between the rooks, turning inexorably, as the rumbling of the massive ships grinding against one another rose in a deafening pitch.

The queen considered the cowboy and the sultana with her mesh eyes. She smiled, gauging the short distance, and raised her stinger: two well-aimed strikes and she would feast again! But her face turned from hungry anticipation to abject pain. Her stinger had become lodged between the turning rims. And then crushed.

"ARRRRRRRRRG!" The queen opened her killing jaws and let out an agonizing shriek so horrible that the sultana closed her eyes tight. The queen was being pulled bodily between the rooks, rotating like gigantic mill wheels. Her abdomen went next, mashed between the rims. The tips of her wings crumpled like paper.

"My arms!" cried the sultana. "I'm too tired!"

"You gotta hang on! Ah!" cried the cowboy. The queen, her mouth gaping in pain, tightened her grip like a vise. If she could not eat them, she would make sure they died with her.

In the terror of the shadow of the rims, the cowboy heard a familiar voice, hollow like a flute.

"Danny Ray!"

That voice—Arlette the cannon! Hers was the muzzle near his head!

"Raise your arm, Danny Ray!" she said.

With a terrible groan, the cowboy pulled up on his wrist until the queen's arm was suspended over the open muzzle of the cannon.

"BOOM!"

A tongue of orange flame shot out. The queen shrieked again as her arm was blown in two, the limp hand falling away from the cowboy's wrist. Her throat gurgled wrathfully and in unmatched fury she shrieked again, the last image Danny Ray had of Her Infernal Majesty before the massive rims devoured her.

And then, she was gone.

Danny Ray clasped his aching arm around the sultana and rested his forehead against the *Hog*'s cold stone. The rope tugged in his hand, lifting them up. The rumbling of the rims became fainter. The sultana let go and scrambled over the top of *Hog*'s wall to safety while Hoodie gripped the cowboy under both arms and heaved him aboard just as the rims mashed together below him.

"Reverse engines!" yelled Captain Quigglewigg into the speaking tube. "*Clackmannon*'s on fire!"

The deck hummed as *Hog* wrenched away from *Clackmannon*'s flaming deck, where the form of the commodore emerged from the smoke, his crimson cloak dirty and torn. He stared directly at the cowboy.

There came a bright flash and a terrible BOOOOOOOM! Another explosion, splitting the air like a thunderbolt. *Hog* shook even more violently. Debris shot up into the sky as the *Clackmannon* disintegrated before their eyes. Pieces of charred wood and stones pelted down onto *Hog*'s deck.

"*Clackmannon*—she's blowed up!" Hoodie Crow whistled, shielding his head with his arms.

"Mr. Piper, cease fire!" called Captain Quigglewigg. "But keep 'em primed and run out if you please!"

One more PLOP! was heard as something light hit the deck. Mr. Piper walked over and retrieved it, then smiled as he handed it to the cowboy. "Missing a boot, Danny Ray?"

"Six bells!" called a sailor, amazingly keeping track of his duties through all the confusion and mayhem.

It felt darn good to be back aboard *Hog*!

The prince handed him his cowboy hat and said to Her Highness, "Sultana, are you all right?"

She took the cowboy's injured wrist gently in her hands and then laid her head on his shoulder. "I am now," she sighed.

✳ 17 ✳

The Red Bats

 The prince of Elidor stood at the new steerage wheel, his feet spread wide apart as Hoodie Crow loomed behind him, instructing him on steering the massive rook. He beamed with pleasure as *Hog* flew like the wind: nearly forty knots by the captain's calculations. Wild wind whirled wickedly around the deck, things flapping and slapping that had been thought to be secure.

Captain Quigglewigg focused his glass back eastward. Two rooks and a bishop pursued *Hog* in the distance: *Gallovidian, Sannox Bay*, and *Black Widow*.

"So, we haven't lost the pirates," came a voice at the captain's side. There stood the groggy cowboy.

"Well, hello, Danny Ray!" exclaimed Captain Quigglewigg. "Ah, yes! The hound chases the fox! Notice I don't say the fox chases the rabbit, for *Hog* is no rabbit! We have been crafty, cunning, and carnivorous! *Vulture, Wick*, and *Clackmannon* were more than just lettuce and carrots, ha, ha, ha!"

Mr. Piper, his arm in a sling, smiled at the cowboy. "You slept away most of the day, Danny Ray. Well-deserved rest, though!"

"Tell me later what happened to you two," remarked the captain, looking at him curiously. Then he put his arm around the cowboy and said, "After you and the sultana were kidnapped aboard *Clackmannon*, the pirates quit fighting and sailed off into the fog. Queerest thing I ever saw, them not following up their advantage. Well, we couldn't very well let them snatch our favorite lubberick and get clean away, seeing how you steered ol' *Hog* through the fog like a hero! So we followed the pirates at a distance while making repairs to *Hog* as best we could."

"How did you follow *Clackmannon* in the fog, sir?"

"With this!" said Piper, displaying the Heart of Ildirim in the palm of his hand.

"I'm sure glad you guys showed up," said Danny Ray, nodding in thanks. He laid his hat back and the wind tore at his hair. "Boy! *Hog*'s a real hot rod with these clabbernappers!"

Quigglewigg shot him a questioning glance and said, "D'ye mean a hot rod to press out the ruffles of your shirt?"

"No." Danny Ray frowned. "I mean like a hot rod race car with a souped-up engine!"

"Souped-up?" asked the captain with a start. "The engine? Danny Ray, how can soup and engines be combined so?"

"Aw shucks, sir!" laughed Danny Ray, and then he said, "Never mind!" The cowboy leaned against the cold stone rim and took a deep breath. He missed home; Diesel, his dog; his brothers; hamburgers, pizza, and a cold Coke; he even missed the red dirt of eastern Oklahoma.

"Well, looky there!" Captain Quigglewigg said, pursing his lips. He focused his telescope on the pursuing pirate ships. A long crimson commodore's pennant streamed out from *Gallovidian*.

"That ol' Sarksa commodore is harder to kill than a cockroach!" Danny Ray grimaced.

"D'ye see the prince there, steering the rook?" asked Piper.

"Yeah, I saw him," replied Danny Ray flatly. The prince laughed and stuck out his tongue good-naturedly. The cowboy turned his back and followed Quigglewigg's worried glance beyond the stern of the ship. "Captain, you think the pirates know where we're headed?"

"Don't see how they could," replied Quigglewigg, "but we need to shake them—and soon!"

The captain scratched his green sideburns as the blue and red stern lights of *Hog* sputtered and came on, flashing brightly, signaling the setting of the sun.

"Those lights give me an idea, sir," said Danny Ray. "Can we rig up another set?"

"Don't see why not," replied Quigglewigg, raising an eyebrow.

"Good. Let's say we string out a length of cable as wide as the stern and hang two Bengal red lights on either end, and one starfire blue in the middle. Then bring up the red bats."

"Ha!" chuckled Piper. "It may just fool 'em, Danny Ray!"

The pair of red bats were large and more frightening when up on the main deck. Not a single hair did they have on their wings, but a tough, leathery hide. They reminded Danny Ray of some of the flying dinosaurs he had seen in the museum, except for their furry bodies, their pug noses, and their pointed ears. One of them cast its yellow eyes his way, and then it reached up with a black talon and scratched its head.

The cable was laid out near the back rim, out of sight of the pirates, and the three lights attached. Several of the crew grinned toothlessly at the captain and nudged each other, enjoying the game.

The cowboy decided to go see if the sultana was awake. He descended a staircase into the windy rear gun deck, where the red and blue lights glowed from the stern. Danny Ray heard voices above the wind. A gang of gargoyles appeared, holding the pale sultana and the prince.

"Well, well, well," said JimmJack, their leader, coming forward to face Danny Ray. "It's the O'world warlock. Fancy bumpin' into you down 'ere where it's all quiet, lonely, and dark-like, where the cap'n and none o' his cronies is nosin' around. We got your witch and your little sprig o' royalty." JimmJack motioned to the sultana and the prince.

Danny Ray crossed his arms and stood his ground. "What the heck you doing?"

"Same thing as you did to ol' GrumpleJixx," snarled JimmJack.

"That was an accident!" snapped Danny Ray. "*Hog* took off, sudden-like, and he fell off the back rim. I was there—I know!"

"That's right, you was there!" growled JimmJack, his voice quavering with fury. "You and the unlucky witch here. But you ain't gonna be 'ere fer long, is you? And then, with you gone, ol' *Hog* sails fer home!"

"You're in a peck of trouble!" said Danny Ray, his arms still crossed. "Why don't you just—"

"Hear that, boys?" interrupted JimmJack, wearing a lop-sided grin. "The warlock 'ere says we'm bein' in some trouble!"

The gargoyles laughed mischievously and Danny Ray's blood ran cold as JimmJack unsheathed the prince's sword and pointed it at the cowboy.

"Watch out, Jacky," said one of the mob, "don't know what O'world spells as he can cast on us!"

"Nah, I watched this one fer a while, I 'ave," said JimmJack slyly, catching sight of Danny's blue rope gleaming in the darkness. "Seems to me ol' kowsboy 'ere ain't in no position to tell nobody nothin'—ain't that right, kowsboy?"

The gargoyles howled wickedly.

"You better let us go!" said the prince, puffing out his chest.

"I am the ruler of Port Palnacky, Guardian of the North!" announced the sultana in a weak voice. "I will have you all thrown in the dungeon!"

"But we ain't in Palnacky, is we, witch?" said the little gargoyle, shaking her wrists.

Suddenly the prince bolted away to the other end of the stern, but one of the mob chased him down.

"Get your hands off of me!" raged the prince.

"Maybe it's a hangin' job, Jacky," said another gargoyle, watching the prince struggle with his captor.

"Nah," said JimmJack with a sly grin. "We'm give 'em a choice: Windows or stairs—which will it be, mate?"

"What are you talkin' about?" the cowboy asked angrily.

"Easy way or nasty way," the gargoyle said, motioning with the sword, the blade flashing in the dim light. "Does we throws you outta the back window here, save us a lot of work and clean up; or does we throws you down the stairs, back and forth all the way o' the bottom? Choice is yers!"

WHAP! WHAP! WHAP! A loud beating of wings rent the air as two black masses filled the open space—the red bats! They hovered there momentarily, lowering themselves bit by bit until their darkened lights came to just above *Hog*'s glowing stern lights.

Poof! The stern lights went out. Danny Ray's heart pounded. One thing he had learned from his scrape with the Sarksa queen: When a way of escape presents itself, you'd better take it! In the total blackness, in that split second before the bats' lights went on, Danny Ray grabbed the sultana's hand and sprinted past the startled gargoyles, jumping up on the edge of the stern looming a hundred and fifty feet above the Checkered Sea. The undulating back of one of the bats was just below them.

Poof! On went the lights! The gargoyles could clearly see Danny Ray and the sultana standing up on the rim, silhouetted against the red and blue glow of the new lights.

"At 'em, boys!" shrieked JimmJack, waving his knife, and the pack of gargoyles yammered, tripping over themselves to get at them.

Danny Ray's eyes opened wide with fright as he gripped the sultana's hand.

And jumped.

The air whistled, mixing with the screaming of the sultana;

then came a jarring impact so severe that Danny saw a flash of
white light and felt a jab of pain from biting his tongue—and
the feel of slick, soft fur in his fist. His other hand draped over
the bat, barely holding on to the sultana's hand as he pulled
himself up on the back of the beast.

"Danny!" the sultana screamed. Her feet kicked frantically as
her blanket wound down out of sight into the gulf of darkness.

And then, horribly, her hand slipped.

Time seemed to stand still. Her terrified, unbelieving eyes
met Danny Ray's. His mouth opened in a shout and he lunged,
a desperate grab, keeping his legs tight around the bat. He
caught her arm at the wrist and squeezed so tight that she
gasped.

"If you drop me," she said, her teeth flashing white against
the surrounding darkness, "I'll—I'll never forgive you!"

"I wouldn't," Danny Ray puffed, pulling her up behind him.
"I wouldn't dream of it, Your Highness."

Amid the howling wind and the thunderous beat of leather
wings, the sultana hugged Danny Ray around the waist, afraid
to open her eyes.

"Look!" Danny Ray hooted, laughing like a madman and
pointing. The sultana followed his gaze. On the back of the
other red bat, flying beside them thirty yards away, sat the
dazed prince. A glowing starfire-blue light dangled on the cable in the void between them.

Ahead, the darkened *Hog* drew steadily away from the bats,
disappearing into the night.

"Don't pinch," came a low, gravelly voice, "or I'll drop yer
on yer head!"

"Who said that?" asked an amazed Danny Ray.

"Me's who said it!" The red bat turned his head sideways, a gleaming yellow eye taking in the cowboy and his riding companion. "I don't need no patch o' hair missin'!"

Danny lightened up on his grip and shouted in the bat's ear, "I'm Danny Ray! And this here is the Sultana Sumferi Sar from Port Palnacky!"

"Don't give a fig fer yer names," snarled the bat, "but I ain't deaf!" After another beat of his wings, the bat added, "My name's Shadowdancer, and she over there, me sister, Moonskimmer. You rid bats before, is you?"

"No, just horses," said Danny Ray. "But I sure like this a whole lot better. Don't much like the idea of falling off. It's a long way down there!"

"I dursn't not let that happen!" said the bat. "Hold on, just, you and the missus!"

The prince's mount swung around on a long arc, keeping the tension on the cable. They were now flying south. Danny Ray looked back over his shoulder. Through the sultana's wildly blowing hair he saw the pirate ships signaling to each other, slowing down and turning south toward them, pursuing what they thought were the stern lights of *Hog*. The pirates had taken the bait!

Danny Ray felt the sultana's chin on his shoulder, her lips brushing against the side of his neck.

For a considerable while, the bats flew south. As the sun began to rise, Shadowdancer's breathing became more labored.

BOOM! went a cannon, followed by another. The pirate ships had gained considerably on them, and they began shooting at what they thought was *Hog*. Shadowdancer screeched a signal to his sister and they let go of the cable. The lanterns fell away into the blackness below, followed by a brilliant flash of light and a loud crash marking where they had burst against the hard surface of the Checkered Sea.

"Hang on, just!" cried Shadowdancer as he leaned on his vast eastward wing, turning to the left while Moonskimmer, bearing the prince, veered right, falling away to the west.

BOOM! BOOM! BOOM! The pirates had spotted the bats, realizing they had been tricked. A blurry, heated object hummed close over the cowboy's head, making him stagger— a cannonball!

BOOM! BOOM! Danny Ray saw another cannonball, a round black mass against the pink sky, passing well behind them. Boom! Boom! Boom! Boom! The cannons were farther away now, trying for a lucky shot.

And then it happened.

Shadowdancer lurched violently to one side. Danny Ray and the sultana were almost thrown from his back.

"Me leg! Hit!" cried Shadowdancer. "Hang on!"

The bat staggered, beating his wings to regain altitude. There was no use in Danny Ray asking if they could help. He patted Shadowdancer on the back as the bat sent out another high-pitched signal. The dark flapping shape of Moonskimmer joined them on the right. The prince waved weakly while the bats talked in their native speech.

Northwest they flew, on and on, until the horizon flamed orange. Shadowdancer grew weaker by the minute.

"Need . . . need rest," breathed the great bat. He stopped

beating his wings and began to glide downward, sinking lower, lower, lower.

"We're gonna crash!" shouted Danny Ray. He felt the sultana tighten her arms around him, not a panicky squeeze but a loving, caring embrace. She laid her head on his back, not wanting to witness their awful death.

But at the last moment, Shadowdancer leveled out, skimming the surface of the smooth marble sea, and then agonizingly winged his way into the air again. Moonskimmer flew with them the whole time, like an identical shadow keeping company with her brother.

"There's *Hog*!" The sultana pointed.

The old rook glowed pink in the light of the rising sun. Figures running on the deck pointed and trained telescopes on them as Moonskimmer flew on ahead and landed on *Hog*'s rim, much to the relief of a tired and weary prince.

"Shadowdancer!" urged Danny Ray. "You can do it! We're almost there!"

But Shadowdancer had lost too much blood. His wings beat slower and slower, as if the sighting of *Hog* had sapped his last reservoir of strength. The bat's head lolled back and forth as he leaned from side to side, trying to remain conscious.

Closer, closer they drew to the rook. Several of *Hog*'s crew members scattered from the wall as Shadowdancer skimmed overhead. The giant bat made a torturous gurgling sound as he flapped his wings in one last tremendous upward beat, caught the air firmly, and paused in midair, settling heavily on the rook's deck.

The crew erupted into a rousing chorus of cheers.

"Danny Ray!" Mr. Piper waved with his good arm. Behind the master gunner loomed Hoodie Crow, a grim smile playing across his dark features.

"Well done!" cried Captain Quigglewigg, saluting up at him.

"What's wrong, Danny Ray?" whispered the sultana, leaning forward and kissing him on the cheek, finding it wet with tears.

The cowboy ruffled Shadowdancer's cinnamon-colored fur.

"Is he—?" asked Moonskimmer, perched nearby.

Danny Ray nodded.

Moonskimmer let out a long, strangled cry.

☀ 18 ☀

Blackguard Mutiny

 The sun was setting when a newly awakened Danny Ray and prince felt their way out onto *Hog's* deck. The sultana sat in a canvas chair rigged up for her by Hoodie Crow.

"Morning," nodded the cowboy.

"You mean, good evening!" she smiled, looking at the prince and holding out a shiny object. "I have a surprise for you!"

"My sword!"

"JimmJack and his foul friends are below in irons!" she said.

The prince assumed the posture of a scarecrow, holding out his arms to either side.

"He expects you to buckle the sword on him," said Danny Ray with a shake of his head.

"I am a sultana!" she said haughtily. "I don't dress anyone!"

"You guys are too much!" sighed the cowboy. "Here, give it to me."

As Danny Ray reached the silver belt around his waist and

clasped it, real delight spread over the prince's features and he affectionately patted the hilt of his sword.

A smiling Mr. Piper and a group of gunners happened by and slapped the cowboy on the back. But there was another group of sailors huddled around the exact spot where Shadow-dancer had fallen, speaking quietly and glancing the cowboy's way with sullen looks.

"Jack-a-lack! Jack-a-lack," they said, chanting a song over and over that went like this:

"Jack-a-lack!
Jack-a-lack!
Here's a potion
Don't come back!

Find a way!
Mind a way!
Here's a charm
To keep from harm!
Tail of wolf!
Nail of wolf!
Round my neck
To charm the deck!

Jack-a-lack!
Jack-a-lack!
Here's a potion
Don't come back!"

Danny Ray shook his head and snorted. "What's all that commotion about? Every song in this whole doggoned world is nutty! Jack-a-lack! Sounds like a girl's jump-ropin' song!"

The prince laughed in his turn.

"Keep your voices down—both of you!" cautioned the sultana. Her earrings caught the red reflection of the fading sun as she met the cowboy's blue eyes. "Not everyone is overjoyed that we returned safely! I can't take too much more excitement!"

The prince wiped his mouth as if he were going to say something, and then laughed again.

"Besides," said the sultana, with a raised eyebrow, "the songs from Oklahoma aren't ridiculous? I dare you to sing me one, Danny Ray!"

"Me too!" the prince said mischievously, rattling his sword in its scabbard.

"Well, all right then—let me see!" The cowboy shoved his hat back off his forehead and belted out the first tune that came to mind:

"I come from Alabama with
A banjo on my knee,
I'm g'wan to Louisiana
My true love for to see.

It rained all night the day I left
The weather it was dry,
The sun so hot I froze to death
Susanna, don't you cry.

Oh Susanna!
Oh don't you cry for me!
I've come from Alabama with
A banjo on my knee."

Danny Ray folded his arms. "Now, that's a real song!"

"That was beautiful!" said the prince, laying back his head and cackling.

" 'It rained all night—the weather it was dry'?" The sultana smirked. " 'The sun so hot I froze to death'—doesn't that sound ridiculous to you, Danny Ray?"

"You don't know nothing! It's a play on words," he replied, fluttering his hand like a bird. "On purpose-like."

"Maybe." The sultana shrugged. "What is a banjo?"

"It's like a guitar, sort of," Danny Ray said. "You rest it on your leg and strum it with your fingers. Only a banjo's sort of clanky—sounds like marbles rolling down a tin roof."

"How dreadful!" she said.

"It is! It's awful! And my daddy thinks so too! My mom hates the banjo, and so does my aunt, and—well, come to think on it, everyone I know hates the banjo, 'cept my uncle Ed—he plays one but he lives out in Nevada all by his lonesome where nobody hears him play."

"Well, if it's such an awful instrument, why shouldn't Susanna cry for him?" put in the prince, suddenly taking sides with the sultana.

"Hmmm." Danny Ray thought for a moment. "Maybe she don't know any better—"

"Because she's only a girl?" inquired the sultana.

"Shoot, no," replied Danny Ray, "I didn't mean—"

"It ain't proper to interrupt a ghost-chantin', boy!"

A new voice, thick and menacing, broke into their conversation.

It was Black Harry, a huge mountain man with a long black beard and huge forearms like an ape's. He had six fingers and six toes and came to stand over them with a whole group of his friends.

"Aye—bad luck," chimed in GrimmAx, the gargoyle bosun, coming to stand beside Black Harry.

A rough voice issued out of the pack: "And we don't need no worser luck right now!"

The group soon became a mob, sailors gathering on deck from all over the ship.

"Bad enough we'm missing the Mushy Festival up Cricket way," said another voice.

"Yis, yis," nodded GrimmAx, "with mushrooms and doggy sausages and tadpole taters, and bosom frogs sizzlin' on sticks! No, instead we traipsin' all around the world, chasin' a queen what we never seen, and being chased ourselves by pirates!"

The cruel-looking cat was ready in the gargoyle's hand, the knotted ends grazing the deck. He cast a filthy look at the prince, who smiled back, toying with the hilt of his sword.

"What's going on here?" demanded Hoodie Crow, the first lieutenant. He interposed his huge black bulk between Danny Ray and the mob. His downturned horns shone like ebony in the evening light.

Black Harry squared off with him. "Mind yer own business, Hoodie!"

"You're a big bully, Black Harry!" breathed the huge coal-troll, his eyes lighting up a brighter white at the confrontation.

"This ain't none o' your affair!" said another voice from the crowd.

"I'm officer in charge," boomed Hoodie. "This is my watch!"

"Get below with the rest o' the coal-humping maggots!" sneered GrimmAx. "We'm decent, sun-abiding folk."

"Put that cat away, Ax!" bellowed Hoodie Crow.

GrimmAx snarled. "I got this cat out fer protection. From this warlock and his witch what done fer GrumpleJixx; and ol' JimmJack in jail!"

"JimmJack's in jail because he's stupid jest like you, Ax," said Hoodie. "GrumpleJixx, the filthy little deck scrubber, was drinking and fell off the back rim all by hisself."

"That's right!" interjected the prince.

"Shut up, you little muckraker!" boomed Black Harry angrily, displaying a mouth of uneven teeth.

The prince's hand flashed to the hilt of his sword, but then he remembered his promise not to threaten any of the crew.

"You been drinkin' again, Black Harry!" warned Hoodie Crow. "So you best hold your peace! I won't have no rum-blin's, tumblin's, and grumblin's on deck. For shame—you and your humpbacked rat-eater friends a-threat'nin' folks as smaller than you."

"We'm going to do as we please!" hissed GrimmAx.

"Shut yer frog hole," said Hoodie thickly. "We trolls knows how to parboil a gargoyle: roast 'em up fine with a squeeze of lemon—oh, excuse me, Captain!"

Captain Quigglewigg, with Mr. Piper beside him, appeared in their midst in his white evening shirt. The mob of sailors stepped respectfully back. "This has all the signs of a mutinous gathering!" Quigglewigg wiped his chicken greasy hands on a napkin and said, "Someone talk—I'm not going to stand here all night!"

"We'm singin' Jack-a-lack as to ward off ghosts"—GrimmAx's voice was deep and gravelly—"when this little strumpet-cowboy fellow as laughed at us!"

"Cap'n, you knows Buckholly Harbor's haunted, and that's a fact!" put in Black Harry.

A humming of agreement buzzed over the mob.

"There ain't no such thing as ghosts!" snickered Danny Ray. He hooked his thumbs in his front pockets and shook his head. But he immediately regretted it, for the entire crew, the officers, the captain, even the sultana, were as quiet as night.

"I seen a ghost, Mr. Warlock Cowboy, yis, yis," said Grimm-Ax, nodding vigorously. "Prime ghost—up Skallywagg way! Had two eyes—one to the front for where's goin', one in the back o' its head for seein' where it'd been. No sneakin' up on a ghosty like that!"

"Maybe there's no ghosts in the Otherworld, Danny Ray," spoke up the captain, "but what was you a-thinkin' interrupting their ghost-chanting?"

"Don't matter, Cap'n," said a man named Bulldog Jenkins. "We'm goin' to die anyway when the Ghost of Buckholly Harbor gets 'old of us!"

The mob broke out into a chorus of angry shouts and not a few fists were raised in the air.

"Listen to me, men!" Captain Quigglewigg raised his hands to quiet them. "I know we've been caught up in events that none of us could have foreseen, like fighting off pirates and sailing to Buckholly Harbor, but there it is—and we've come through like heroes!

"Black Harry!" Quigglewigg shouted. "I saw you lead the charge behind Hoodie that cut down the *Vulture* pirates before they could kill Danny Ray! Jenkins, it was your gun crew that hammered the *Vulture*, swept her deck clear and caused her to break up on Castle Rock! Joe Bolger!—I see you back there—it was your gun division that blasted *Wick*'s guts out—and I'm grateful to all of you!"

"We'm all loyal blokes," spoke up Bulldog Jenkins, "hearts of oak, loyal and true."

"And you're also men of action!" cried Captain Quigglewigg walking fearlessly among the crew, and they moved aside wherever he went. "When I look about me, whom do I see? I see my old crew of man-o'-wars men, my chosen band of warriors, the destroyers of two bishops and a rook in less than a week! *Vulture* and *Wick* are on the rocks because of you men, and *Clackmannon* will never sail again!"

There arose a fierce growl of approval from the crew.

"I see sailors," continued the captain, "who will do their duty, no matter the cost! I see men who trust their captain, no questions asked!"

Black Harry, so angry a moment before, nodded fiercely.

"Is there a ghost in Buckholly Harbor?" The captain looked out over the silent crowd of sailors. "Is there, now? Doesn't matter! We are sailing in, ghost or no ghost!"

Wild cheering broke out. On and on it went, until the captain raised his arms for silence. "Now, men! This is a quiet part of the world—a watchful place. We don't want to announce our presence! Hands to their stations—quietly, now! Prepare to darken ship. The queen we search for may already be in the harbor ahead of us. Darken ship, I say!"

The mob dispersed. Captain Quigglewigg accepted a telescope from Mr. Piper and scanned the deep blue domes of the Silverlode Mountains. Whether he chose to notice it or not, the prince, the sultana, and Danny Ray gazed at him with something like hero worship.

⁜ 19 ⁜

The Ghost of Buckholly Harbor

 The twinkling lights of Drinkwater passed by, nestled at the foot of the Silverlode Mountains. *Hog* glided by the town like a whisper in the leaves. Hoodie Crow pointed off into the night, conversing with the captain while they followed the mountain range due north. A valley came down to the sea, and *Hog* swung toward it quietly, effortlessly, like a sigh in the wind. A tall monument of rock jutted up from the squares, having a strange human likeness, the face turned toward the open sea.

"That there's the Hopeful Maiden," said Mr. Piper. "Been years since I was here last, but I hear tell what it were a maiden as waited on her beloved—waited so long she turned to stone, as it were."

An abandoned harbor appeared where the black and white squares invaded between two arms of the mountains: Buckholly Harbor.

"Take her in gently," the captain ordered.

Under the smooth power of the clabbernappers, *Hog* floated into the deeper darkness of the inlet. Buckholly Harbor was smaller than Port Palnacky, but a rook or queen could hide here well enough.

Huge gnarled trees with grasping branches watched *Hog* sail by. Old crackling leaves blew across the squares and piled up against Cutty Throats, a small tree-covered island in the center of the harbor. Danny Ray heard a multitude of creaking branches swaying in rhythm in the night breeze.

"If ever there was a ghost in this world," commented the prince, coming up to Danny Ray's elbow, "then this would be his winter palace!"

"No doubt," nodded the sultana.

"Nobody been here for a while." Mr. Piper pointed below, where large spiderwebs stretched and snapped as *Hog* wound her way around the harbor.

"My eyes must be playing tricks on me," said Danny Ray. "The squares are red, not black!"

"Autumn's coming soon," explained Piper. "The squares turn blue in winter, green in spring, and back to black in summer."

Off to one side, a crippled knight chess piece as massive as *Hog* lay on its side, its horse's head crushed. Ancient vines and trees grappled around its throat, those marble eyes having stared up into the stars for countless years. The knight's sculptured frown, suggesting bold gallantry, seemed a cruel mockery. Cracks in its hull revealed rusting gears and steering cables.

"You see them trees what strangles the ol' ship?" said Piper, pointing. "Them's hobbleberry trees. Now's harvest time. If Cap'n's hunch is correct, we'll see ol' *Winter Queen* arrive to reap a crop."

"Hope you're right," replied Danny Ray.

"But sooner better than later," blurted the prince. "I don't much like this place!" He picked up a loose piece of masonry lying beside a cannon's carriage, and flung it off into the trees. A shape rose from the woods and winged its way directly over *Hog*, calling out harshly, and then disappeared over the harbor.

"Dear Prince!" seethed the captain, his voice shaking with fury. "Can you not refrain from your mischievous pranks in this dangerous place? Next time unscrew your head and throw it over the edge!"

A wall, partially hidden in the trees, marched up the hillside to a broken tower overshadowed by an abandoned castle where grappling vines and hoary trees now reigned in the place of kings, of queens, of princes.

"Goll Morna," whispered Piper, clicking his teeth nervously. "'Tis a cursed place, to be sure, of ancient and dark memory, with tales as would make your arm hairs stand up. Unlucky's the day as one sails by this unlucky place."

A strange, eerie sound penetrated the night, not that of the natural creaking of branches nor that of the rustling of leaves, nor still that of the faint humming of the rook's engines, but that of a chanting. A group of gargoyles knelt on *Hog*'s deck, leaning back, hands opened and spread upward. With eyes closed, their sharp mouths moved in unison, reciting a dark liturgy.

"The ol' scrubs is worshipping," mulled Piper under his breath. "Up there, on the castle wall—their brothers, frozen in stone since the War of Judgment."

The gargoyle statues of Goll Morna hunkered down and grimacing, the moonlight playing across their painful features.

A wolf.

It sprang atop an ancient, cracked stone monument marked and defiled with magical designs and with filth runes. The chanting of the gargoyles grew louder. The pale eyes of the wolf, like sick moons, peered down at the harbor, at the *Hog*, at Danny Ray.

A shiver trembled down Danny Ray's spine.

The prince recited the verse:

"Dark is the day, the day of doom
When shines no sun, shines no moon;
A wind's age, a wolf's age
Before the world's ruin."

"It is a verse from a larger poem," he whispered, "concerning the end of the world."

"It's downright creepy!" said Danny Ray. "This whole place is creepy!"

The moon hung suspended over the mountains, and black branches were silhouetted against the white disk. *Hog* had come full circle.

"Slow engines," the captain ordered, looking down over the rim. A tree-lined arm of land hooked out into the harbor near the opening. *Hog* navigated behind the outcropping, sitting on the only square available, her rim sticking up over an old stone wall atop the hill.

"All stop," ordered the captain. The clabbernappers wound down as *Hog* extinguished the rest of her lights except for the binnacle lantern. The ship's masthead was lowered.

"Listen to the wind," whispered one of the gunners to Piper. "Them's threats of wickedness what the trees is planning for us, eh?"

"Threats of cold murder under a lonely moon!" said another.

"Silence in the ship!" said Hoodie Crow. The crew became sullen, even fearful of the brooding forest. The wind fell to just a whisper, the silence from the trees hemming them in.

The captain took a deep breath.

The wait began.

Midnight.

The moon had cleared the mountaintop when a fog came creeping over the deck of *Hog*. It was not a natural fog, the kind in Port Palnacky, but a crawly, creepy fog with gray searching fingers. Danny Ray awakened. Nearby, the prince moaned fitfully with bad dreams. The cowboy stood and let the blanket drop off his shoulders as he joined Captain Quigglewigg at the wheel.

"What is it, sir?" whispered Danny Ray.

The cowboy followed his terrified gaze to a dark mist rising over the rim of *Hog*. Insubstantial as air, it took the more definite shape of a woman, her features, lovely and yet forlorn, with gray tendrils of hair blowing across her face. Upon her head sat a crown, sharp in its detail of leaves and pomegranates. Her gray robe was studded with gems of half-lights that neither sparkled nor beckoned. Her lids opened. Her eyes were colorless and remote, from the world below where all things are cold.

"Who are you?" inquired the captain harshly. "What do you want with us?"

The black-slit eyes of the ghost regarded the captain. Her nose had only one nostril, wide and dark.

"We mean no harm. We are peaceful men," the captain continued in a shaky voice, "on a peaceful mission. I must ask you to state your business!"

The ghost laughed, her teeth gnashing together like long, sharp knives.

"I am hungered." Her voice trailed like the sighing wind. She drew aside the side of her robe to reveal a long sword with a jeweled hilt. "Man's flesh dost I eat, man's blood dost I drink. The bones goeth home." Behind her stood two skull-mungers, bearing necklaces of human skulls around their necks.

The prince came to stand at Danny Ray's side, staring up at the ghost while GrimmAx and the rest of the crew were huddled in fear. Some sailors crouched behind cannons; others had already scampered below the main deck.

Captain Quigglewigg's voice trembled. "Now, see here—"

"Peace!" she crooned, a smile playing about her lips. She tilted her head, and her long, gray hair flowed all the way to the harbor's entrance. "I require only half thy crew. Then thou mayest leave. Perchance, Captain, if thou stayest"—she exer-

cised her ghastly jaws, the teeth grinding together like razors—
"I shall eat all of thy crew. Long hast it been since last I dined
on manflesh!"

"What if we aim to stop you?" asked Danny Ray.

The fell queen laughed. She lifted her arms, and the wind
began to blow and the trees began to moan. With her other
hand she summoned lightning and thunder.

"I possess all power in this place. Thou art in my power:
thou wilt do as I please!" She beckoned, and Danny Ray was
drawn forward, his spurs jangling on the wooden deck. "Thou,
strange little boy, shalt be the first whom I eat. I shall wear thy
teeth on a necklace, just so, like a charm." Her black nails
clicked horribly about her throat.

"Danny Ray!" said Captain Quigglewigg. "Stand back and
let me take care of this!"

"Sir—you heard her!" said the cowboy. He struggled
against invisible chains of steel binding him. "She's ain't going
to let any of us leave lessen she can have half the crew for
supper. Have you chosen the fellers you want to leave behind?"

The captain was silent. Suddenly, Danny Ray had an idea.
"I'll bet I can do something you can't do!"

"No mortal man may match my strength nor my cunning,"
said the ghost of Buckholly Harbor. "Be thou frightened, little
boy, that I make thy death most long and painful."

"It's a bet, then?" asked Danny Ray. "If I can do something
you can't, then you'll skedaddle with your two spooky Hal-
loween friends, and leave us alone?"

The wind eased and the trees became watchful. The harbor

held its breath; the ghost closed her eyes, rolling her head crookedly from side to side as if her neck were broken. The eyes opened. "I am agreed. Thou hast a standing wager from me. Thou hast three trials. If thou loseth all three, all aboard the ship must forfeit their life."

"And if I win?"

"Thou mayest stay in Buckholly Harbor for as long as thou wishest. But, alas, my young, juicy morsel, thou canst not win."

Well, Danny Ray had gotten her this far, but he was at a loss as to what to do next. He was confounded as to what ghosts could or would, couldn't or wouldn't do, but he was willing to give it a try. His hand fell to his belt. All through his adventures his bright blue rope had remained faithful, unnoticed until needed. Danny Ray unwound the coil and set the knot. He waved the rope in the air, around and around, opening and closing his wrist, letting out more of the rope until a large loop whistled over his head. With a quick snap of his wrist he let the rope fly toward one of *Hog*'s cannons.

"Dang!" It was going to fall short! Suddenly the rope lengthened of itself! The lasso caught around the muzzle of one of the brass cannons and Danny Ray pulled it tight and wiped his brow.

The crew erupted into cheers and Danny Ray smiled.

Snap! The ghost tore an old, hoary vine from a nearby tree. It caught fire as the ghost-princess whipped it around her crowned head, snagging one of the cannons, which she yanked from its moorings and flung over the side of the deck. The sound of it crashing far below brought her ghostly eyes back to the cowboy.

"Thou hast two more tries," she said, flicking her black tongue over her lips.

Danny Ray pulled in his rope, thinking. When he had fastened it to his belt, an idea hit him. In a flash, he hopped over onto his hands and raised his feet into the air, performing a perfect handstand.

"Thou hast one last try, and one try only," said the ghost, looking at him upside down from her own handstand. "And for causing me such an inglorious posture, I shall boil thee very thoroughly over a small fire, for weeks. I promise thee!"

Black Harry knelt on the deck nearby, sobbing like a baby.

Fear began to cloud over Danny Ray's courageous heart. In his mind's eye, he was back in Oklahoma.

"Hey boy!" said his daddy's voice. "Now, don't be afraid."

"No, Daddy," said a pint-sized Danny Ray.

A low, gruff snorting came from a nearby pen. There stood a brown bull with a neck as big around as a door. The wine-red eyes of the monster stared at him, daring him to get on his back. His father took him by the hand and led him closer to the pen. Danny Ray's knees shook. The bull snorted again, bulging muscles flexing in his shoulders as he scraped his spiked horns against the metal pipes of the pen.

"You ain't scared, are you, boy?"

"No, sir, I ain't." A knot formed in his throat. "No, sir, I ain't scared at all."

"That's good, Danny Ray, cause one of these days you'll be old enough to ride this feller. When your time comes, they'll yell 'Cowboy up!' and you mount the bull and away you go! If you're scared, that ol' bull—he'll smell it, and you won't have a chance of ridin' him."

"Yes, sir."

Danny Ray looked up at his dad, who put his boot up on the pen and fished in his mouth with a long twig. Overhead, against his black cowboy hat, the clouds soared.

He said, "You remember Uncle Bud, don't you? He got scared, down in San Antonio, and ol' Slingblade stomped all over him. Broke his leg and broke his arm. No, sir, you can't be scared of these devils."

His daddy's face lowered to his. His teeth flashed white as the deep lines of his face split into a grin. "Now, listen, son. It's all right to be scared, but don't show it. That's the real trick. Something will come to mind to help you through it. Got it?"

"Yes, sir," he said in a small voice, rubbing his hands together. "Something will come to mind."

Danny Ray jerked to wakefulness. Then he smiled.

He reached into his vest pocket and withdrew a small square. He carefully unwrapped it and held it up. It was pink! The cowboy placed the square in his mouth and his jaw muscles worked back and forth as he chewed the bright gummy substance.

Danny Ray mumbled, "Hey Captain Quigglewigg, ain't you never seen bubble gum? Your eyes are buggin' out like a stomped-on toad frog!"

The captain went to answer, but the most surprising thing happened! Out of Danny Ray's mouth appeared a large pink orb! The ghost's eyes widened as the bubble grew larger and larger and larger, until—POP!—it disappeared. Danny Ray licked it back into his mouth!

The queen exercised her jaws back and forth, a horrid gurgling issuing from her throat. But it was no use.

"I whipped you fair and square," asserted Danny Ray. "*Hog* can stay here 'til we get our business done, right? You ain't going back on your promise?"

She seethed in silent rage. The trees of Buckholly Harbor rustled and groaned, limbs creaking, cracking, and falling to the ground.

"You shall stay," she said at last. "This shall be the sign of my promise: I shall cover over the moon and her face shalt go black, for her light claweth at me, raketh my soul! But certain death awaiteth thee or any of thy crew that venture forth from this ship. Upon this ship thou shalt abide, or I shall eat thee, bone, blood, and hide."

Then, with a bloodcurdling shriek, this ancient eater-of-blood flew up over the deck, followed by her skull-mungers. The wind shrieked with such fury that Danny Ray wondered whether all the trees in the harbor would be uprooted. Then FLASH!—there came a bolt of light in the sky followed by a faraway rumble of thunder over the distant hills.

Joyous pandemonium broke loose on deck. From every nook and cranny, from every dark place and cubbyhole, from every cupboard and hiding place, cheering Hogs descended on Danny Ray.

Just then, the sultana appeared on deck in her sleeping robe. "My goodness," she said with a yawn. "Did I miss something?"

✻ 20 ✺

Her Majesty, the Queen!

Deep night. Deep silence. Danny Ray slept peacefully in the darkness, dreaming of Oklahoma, of biscuits and flour gravy, of bacon, of grits sprinkled with salt and pepper surrounded by a moat of melted butter, and of the smell of steaming black coffee. A nudging at his elbow brought him out of his deliciously sweet fancies; the warm, savory kitchen air of his dreams was replaced by the chilly, night air of reality; pancakes dripping with syrup were replaced by Piper's face, forefinger to his lips, signaling silence and to follow him.

Danny Ray rolled over out of his blanket, his yellow-and-red shirt black in the darkness. The deck was deserted. The cowboy felt his way to Captain Quigglewigg, standing with Hoodie Crow and the yawning prince. The captain wearily wiped his telescope lens. He had donned his blue hat with the white feather, as if he was confident of action. Mr. Piper handed Danny Ray a telescope with his good hand. The captain startled the cowboy out of his half-sleep.

173

"There," Quigglewigg whispered, pointing out to sea.

Danny Ray was stupid with sleep, and Piper had to nudge him fully awake. The cowboy raised the telescope and scanned the horizon. He saw a glimmer of white, like a feather. His heart thumped wildly as he focused the glass: the shimmering mistress sprang into sharp detail. *Winter Queen* was absolutely breathtaking, with sharply raked lines and a crown of bitter white spikes.

"She's sailing in on the long diagonal," said Hoodie Crow in a low voice. "Largest chess piece I've ever seen!"

The captain gauged the top of the hill concealing them. "We'll be hidden from the queen as she sails past to the back of the harbor. But if she looks back, she'll be able to see our top half. Don't think she'll spot us with the moon hidden, unless her lookout is very, very sharp."

"She's slowed, sir," observed Hoodie Crow.

"She might suspect something's wrong, that we're here," worried the prince.

"No," said Captain Quigglewigg. "Like us, she's probably debating the wisdom of sailing into a haunted harbor."

"But she needs them hobbleberries," commented Mr. Piper, with a wry smile playing across his freckled features, "or she wouldn't be here in the first place—good advice what we got back in 'Nacky."

"Easy!" the captain cautioned. He brought up his telescope. "Everyone crouch down by the front rim," he whispered. "Here she comes—Her Majesty, the Queen!"

A faint rumbling like distant thunder announced the

queen's arrival. A massive white crown appeared over the tops of the trees. *Winter Queen* floated into the harbor like a dream. Her lookouts, as Quigglewigg had predicted, were totally unaware of the rook tucked back off to the side of the harbor entrance.

Danny Ray peeked from his hiding place, staring with openmouthed fascination as the queen sailed past, flashes of blue and red emanating from her stonework as if she had been fashioned of arctic ice by snow giants. Green and violet lights flashed around her lofty crown.

"I used to throw rocks from up there," commented the prince with an upturned face.

"Ain't hard to believe you'd do that!" replied the cowboy.

"Quiet there!" growled Hoodie Crow.

Everyone had the same expression—awestruck; not only by her beauty but by the queen's presence: the most powerful chess piece on the sea.

"My goodness!" exclaimed the sultana, appearing like magic in a crouch beside the cowboy. This time she had slept in her traveling clothes, not daring to miss any of the action.

"Your Highness," the captain said with a bow of his head.

Even newly awakened, the sultana was beautiful, perhaps even more so. She rubbed the sleep out of her eyes as *Winter Queen* dropped anchor at the far end of the harbor, the tall island covered with trees helping to shield *Hog. Winter Queen's* helm lights faded as the sound of the powerful zanzoomies wound down. Her crew began the arduous task of gathering hobbleberries.

"The good news is we've found her and that surprise is on our side," Captain Quigglewigg said, standing up. He peered out at *Winter Queen* across the harbor. "The bad news is, capturing her will be quite risky."

Danny Ray squinted, measuring the opening of the inlet and the large harbor area. He said, "We're going to block the entrance with *Hog* and make her fight, right, sir?"

The reaction he saw in the captain's eyes told him he was not only wrong, but delirious as well.

"Do you reckon what a chess piece that size and power would do to *Hog*, Danny Ray?" said the captain, dumbstruck.

"She'd knock us clean back to Port Palnacky!" assured Hoodie Crow, his white eyes flashing.

"With only one bounce in between!" added Piper.

Danny Ray studied the queen's twinkling crown in the distance. Captain Quigglewigg was right: *Winter Queen* was way too large and well armored for *Hog* to tangle with. And they could hardly climb down and run across the harbor to board her. She'd be sure to see them. Ridiculous thought!

The captain motioned Hoodie Crow and the crew around him. "All right, men, I mean to cut out *Winter Queen* yonder while she's busy loading her hobbleberries. It's our only chance. We'll need two crews, cutlasses and grappling hooks—but quietly about our work, eh? The smallest noises skip like stones across the harbor! Hoodie, I trust the ramp doors are well oiled—both pawns ready to disembark?"

The huge first lieutenant nodded and knuckled his forehead.

The captain said curtly, "Well, let's at it!"

Buckholly Harbor lay dark beneath a thick veil of cloud. The preoccupied queen had no idea that *Hog*'s two pawns, *Minnow* and *Midget*, having been quietly released from the rook's lower deck, even now sailed side by side across the harbor toward her.

The pawns were small, a fourth the size of *Hog*, and each sported a huge globe rising conspicuously out of the center of its deck. Although the pawns sailed only one square at a time, they arrived quickly at the tree-covered island in the center of the harbor, without once alerting the queen to their presence. There was little fear of discovery from *Winter Queen* as long as they stayed hidden from sight by Cutty Throats Island.

Danny Ray stood on the deck of *Minnow* holding on to a large unlit lantern resting atop the front rim. The surface of the sea was much nearer than it had been when he stood on the lofty battlements of the mother ship, *Hog*.

Hoodie Crow nodded to Danny Ray. The cowboy gripped the shutter of a signal lantern and flicked it open and shut, open and shut. *Midget*, commanded by Mr. Piper, acknowledged with a red light, and the pawns separated, sailing in opposite directions toward either end of the island. Hoodie took a deep breath. No turning back now, he brooded solemnly.

But then, just as the pawns were about to clear the trees and converge on the queen from both directions, disaster struck.

KAAAW-YEE! KAAAW-YEE! KAAAW-YEE! came a harsh cry. Wings fluttered so close over Danny Ray's head that he instinctively ducked. The same black winged shape that had

flown over them when first *Hog* had sailed into the harbor
called out its harsh alarm. It flew off toward the island and
vanished in the tangle of black branches.

"Stop engines!" urged Hoodie Crow in a stifled cry. The
low hum of the little bobberkin, the pawn's single dynamo no
larger than a man's fist, slowed *Minnow* to a stop.

The cowboy could barely discern the orb and spiked turret
of *Winter Queen* peeking above the top of the trees. But what
he saw alarmed him. Her crystal top-knob began to glow as a
pure white searchlight flowed out over the harbor and the
trees, searching for the source of the disturbance.

"Duck down!" said Danny Ray. The sailors crouched behind *Minnow's* sheltered rim just as a heavy, almost liquid
white light flooded through the trees and fell directly upon
them. That danged bird, cursed Danny Ray. It had betrayed
their hiding place!

"The queen—she's saw us!" growled Hoodie Crow. The
light slid over them again.

"Hoodie! Wait!" cautioned Danny Ray. "Stay where you are!"

The spotlight hovered overhead briefly, then swept on. In-
credibly, they had just enough tree cover that the queen had
not spotted *Minnow* or *Midget*!

"That we was lucky!" sighed Hoodie Crow.

Danny Ray bit his lip nervously as her powerful search
beam began to scan the harbor, following the coastline farther
back to where *Hog* lurked. It was only a matter of time until—
oh no! The rook was fully lit up, only partially hidden by the
distant tree-lined hill. The light steadied, stopped there.

"We'm done for!" whined a sailor. "*Hog's* been spotted!"

✦ 21 ✦

At the End of Your Rope

 Danny Ray had expected to hear *Winter Queen*'s zanzoomies roaring to life, and for her to attempt a desperate run for the harbor entrance. But then, amazingly, the searchlight passed on. It swept back uncertainly to shine on *Hog*. Then the powerful beam swept inquisitively toward the opposite coastline. Finally, the light flashed out and the harbor was drowned in darkness.

"What was that all about, Hoodie?" asked Danny Ray.

Hog's first lieutenant chuckled and said, "*Winter Queen* seen what she wanted to see: a woodsy hillside topped by a crumbly wall and an old gray tower. She thinks *Hog* is what's left of a watchtower near the entrance! If *Hog* was a gleamin' new rook, like Cap'n Quiggs and I have always wanted, well, we'd be in trouble right now. For the first time I'm glad *Hog* is a rambly, grambly old rook. She blends in real nice, don't she, with that old wall—it saved her, and us. Aha!"

Hoodie Crow sprang up, looming huge against the starry sky.

"Well, men," he whispered hoarsely, "our plan to capture

the queen still stands! Most of *Winter Queen*'s crew will be
ashore gathering them hobbleberries. And she don't have no
cannon, remember. So, as the cap'n says, Let's at it!" Hoodie
winked and added, "Danny Ray, take the helm."

The cowboy nodded. If he had had nerve enough to steer a
huge rook through the fog with pirates all around, he just
might be trusted with steering a pawn!

Hoodie signaled and the crew vanished to their appointed
stations, ready to carry out the final and most dangerous part
of the mission.

Danny Ray felt a strong vibration through the steerage
wheel—the little bobberkin kicking in as they sailed around
the headland of the island. The terrifying beauty of the queen
loomed in front of them, glittering, glowing, towering in the
darkness.

"Can't see Mr. Piper yet," muttered Hoodie as he raised his
night telescope and peered into the darkness. "Could be a
good sign, though. If we can't see *Midget*, neither can the
lookouts on *Winter Queen*."

Danny Ray wasn't so sure. Maybe *Midget* had grounded on
the far side of the island and even now was desperately trying
to extricate herself. Or maybe she had had engine troubles. Or
maybe she had lost her way in the darkness. Or—

"Confounded miseries!" exclaimed Hoodie.

Danny Ray followed his gaze overhead. The moon started
to peek out from the edge of her dark confinement.

Of course! The ghost of Buckholly Harbor had promised
to veil the moon only as long as the crew stayed on *Hog*.
Danny Ray's thoughts instinctively went to the shadowy

winged creature with the loud, terrible cry. The bird had warned the ghost of *Hog*'s arrival in the harbor last evening, and now it had told her that the terms of her covenant with *Hog* had been violated. A chill ran down the cowboy's spine as he considered what that meant.

"We don't have much time, Hoodie!" said Danny Ray.

The moon asserted itself in full, glowing down wickedly white, lighting up the harbor with a pale, strange luminosity. At once, the ships leaped into sharp detail.

"There's Piper!" snapped GrimmAx the gargoyle, pointing with his cutlass. "Look at *Midget* fly!"

Midget was already up to the queen, angled at her from behind. Her crew stood with grappling hooks, getting ready to board the queen.

Tweeeeeeeeeeel! Tweeeeeeeeeeel! A sharp piercing whistle sounded from *Winter Queen*. Bright warning lights flashed around the queen's lofty crown. Torches hurried along her crystal battlements. The rumbling of her zanzoomies started up, growing louder and louder, breaking the quiet of the harbor as the powerful ship awakened.

"These'll come in handy," said Hoodie with a grin, handling a wicked-looking grappling hook. It had long, sharp, clawlike fingers, with barbs along the main post where the rope attached. "Picked these whistlers off *Hog*'s wall after *Vulture* blew up."

Danny Ray fidgeted impatiently with his grip on *Minnow*'s helm as he watched *Midget* nudge against the *Winter Queen*'s side. *Whirrr! Whirrr! Whirrr!* sounded the grappling hooks as they sailed overhead and fastened themselves on the queen's crown. Now Danny Ray understood why Hoodie had called them whistlers.

Minnow was still too far off but Danny Ray could make out Mr. Piper, injured arm and all, scaling the queen's sheer walls with the other Hogs, hallooing and shouting as they pulled and kicked and heaved and scrambled their way up the sides of the queen.

"It's *Minnow*'s turn!" hollered Hoodie Crow to his crew. "Prepare to board! Steer handsomely, Danny! Lay us alongside!"

Hoodie, with his wooden leg, thumped up on *Minnow*'s front rim along with the rest of the crew waiting for their chance to board. Hoodie swung his hook around his head with his hefty arms, around and around, the hook whistling madly in an ever widening circle. He let it fly at what was still a tremendous distance to the queen.

KER-CLANK!

The hook grabbed hold of the queen, and Hoodie swung off the wall as the sailors sent up a chorus like howling murder.

All of Piper's boarders were away. Danny Ray was awed by the spectacle, Hogs streaming up the walls to the very crown or ducking into open portholes along the way, like scavenging ants exploring an alien anthill. Far overhead, the top-knob of *Winter Queen* was haloed like a saint by the full moon.

Suddenly, the cowboy felt the cold steel of a knife against his ribs.

GrimmAx's fanged mouth almost touched Danny Ray's face as he said, "Thought I forgot 'bout you, eh, cowboy?"

The *Midget*'s crew had their backs turned to the steerage wheel, concentrating on the queen as she loomed larger and larger. Some of them had begun to twirl their grappling hooks.

"If you cry out I'll 'ave your liver on the end o' my sticker, see?" The gargoyle smiled, enjoying the shock and terror on the cowboy's face. But Danny Ray knew everything depended his steering *Minnow* alongside the queen. He couldn't quit the helm and let the Hogs down.

And GrimmAx knew it.

"What's a matter, warlock boy?" he asked through gritted teeth. "Bit o' dilemma, eh? I tried feedin' you alive to the pirates but I'd be a lyin' booby to say I won't enjoy slittin' you open myself! Oh yeah, you jest figgurin' it out? It was me, GrimmAx, as hit you in the back o' the head when the *Clackmannon* pirates boarded us!"

Danny Ray felt the knife tense, ready to jab deeply. "Here's for GrumpleJixx and ol' JimmJack, my *brother*!"

But the look of murderous satisfaction on the gargoyle's face changed to horror as a huge sword thrust its bloody point out through his chest.

The gargoyle was lifted off his feet, rising like a twitching, gesticulating puppet suspended in midair. But the ancient blade that pierced GrimmAx was no more ancient than the black-nailed hand that pulled him off that spitlike blade, that raised him to a gaping mouth. The ghost of Buckholly Harbor's one nostril flared as, with a horrifying sound, her teeth closed down around the gargoyle's head, snapping it off like an icicle. With another gruesome, bone-crunching squeeze, her jaws widened to swallow him whole.

The crew scattered from *Minnow*'s rim, screaming in terror and letting fall their hooks and swords as the ghost finished her grisly meal.

The slitted eyes of the ghost did not regard the fleeing sailors, numerous as they were; there would be time to dine on them later. Her head turned, her eyes falling with fury on the boy holding the steerage wheel, the child of the Other-world who had caused her so much embarrassment, the cowboy who had been the only one, over eons and eons of time, to outwit her.

As the battle raged along *Winter Queen*'s battlements, the ghost drifted toward Danny Ray. He backed away from *Minnow*'s helm until he found himself pinned against the rim of the pawn. *Minnow* lost her way, drifting off course.

"First the appetizer, then the main course," the ghost crooned in a blood-chilling fashion.

"My meat's a little stringy," replied Danny Ray.

"I shall boil thee in thine own heart's blood until thou art tender," she smiled.

The cowboy climbed up on the edge of the pawn's rim, the heels of his boots sticking out over a fifty-foot drop above the marble sea. Out of the corner of his eye, he saw the base of *Winter Queen* tremble with power, straining against her brake. She was going to try to shake the boarders off her sides with a massive jolt forward, and then sail swiftly out the harbor entrance before *Hog* might intervene.

Think! Danny Ray scolded himself. Think! as he unfas-

tened his rope with shaky hands. He could hardly breathe and
his heart pounded. His whole body trembled. I'll only get one
chance, he thought as the looped end of rope danced on top of
the toes of his cowboy boots.

And it's gotta count!

The rope felt good in Danny Ray's hand. It whistled softly
above his head as he twirled it, the thin, blue serpent shimmering in the fading moonlight.

"What dost thou do?" mused the ghost. She drew closer, the
deep rage flashing in her eyes. "Entwine me if thou wilt! Bring
me unto thyself, my next and choicest meal!"

Winter Queen released her brake with a wrenching POP!,
nudging *Midget* out of the way. The *whoosh! whoosh! whoosh!*
of Danny Ray's rope was drowned in the sudden roar of
Winter Queen. In a blaze of white, in a rush of terrifying
wind like that of a white hurricane, *Winter Queen* roared
down on *Minnow*, which had drifted directly, fatally into her
path.

But at that split second, in the howling wind and rumbling
chaos, Danny Ray cast his rope in a long arching throw that
caught one of the side spikes of the queen's crown.

Hold on! he told himself. Hold on!

With a shriek the ghost rushed at Danny Ray. Her razorlike
nails flashed and slashed, and just as her scissors-sharp grasp
closed down upon him, Danny Ray vanished.

"WHOOOOAHHHHHH!" he shouted as he was whipped
off the deck of *Minnow*. Roping an ornery bull was one thing.
But roping a stampeding queen two hundred and fifty feet
high and weighing thousands of tons was something else!

Danny Ray closed his eyes and held on for dear life, swinging out into the night air. Below him, in a flash of light and a terrible BOOM!, *Minnow* disintegrated with the ghost of Buckholly Harbor still aboard.

"See ya laaaaater, ghosty!" sang Danny Ray as he sailed through the air.

But he had spoken too soon.

From out of that cloud of destruction, from out of the shower of burning wood and sulfurous brick that had only seconds before been a pawn, the ghost flew madly toward the cowboy with eyes blazing, her sword drawn, her fell crown catching the fading moonlight. Danny Ray was too busy being terrified of the ghost to notice how high up he was, with only a rope between him and a funeral.

Winter Queen gathered speed as she flew toward the harbor opening. But she sailed not nearly so fast as to outrun the ancient specter haunting that harbor.

"Yikes!" yelled Danny Ray. The rope of thrillium jerked him up just as the ghost made a savage lunge at the cowboy.

Whoom! The ghost's sword stroke slashed just over the astonished cowboy, twanging against the rope.

"Oh no!" Danny Ray thought as he felt the stinging vibration in his hands. The blade came slashing down again against the rope. Twang! The ghost howled with fury. Danny Ray hooted. No blade—no matter whose—is sharp enough to cut through thrillium!

Winter Queen's sudden jerking shift in direction swung Danny Ray sideways. He raised his boots in the air, skimming the dark treetops with the ghost in pursuit, her robes fluttering and flowing in the wind. Off to the east, the sky began to pale.

The trees cleared; he swung out over the harbor again. Danny Ray glanced below. It was *Hog*! *Winter Queen* thundered by so close that Quigglewigg and the sultana fell backward, the steerage wheels spinning wildly! The prince cried out in dismay.

"Ah!" Danny Ray grimaced as a black hand reached out and seized his arm like a vise.

"Thou wouldst leave my harbor without saying farewell?" leered the ghost through clenched, knife-sharp teeth. Her grip tightened and she cackled horribly and shook the cowboy. "Ah! Ill-mannered boys are good-tasting boys!"

But suddenly the ghost let go her grip, her grim features turning to surprise as a well-aimed kick in the stomach sent her whirling away. The cowboy glanced down.

"Prince!" he shouted out in surprise. "Where—where did you come from?"

"Grabbed the rope, the end of the rope, as it—as it flew over *Hog*. Sorry I—Oh!"

Winter Queen cleared the harbor entrance and accelerated out into the open sea. Danny Ray's hat whipped off his head and dangled around his neck by the chinstrap. He held on with a death grip, swinging with the prince like a clock's pendulum.

"Ohhhh! I'm going to die!" shouted the prince above the wind. "I'm going to die! I'm going to die! Ohhhh!"

"Don't worry!" Danny Ray called down to the prince. "The rope has a way of grabbing your hands and not letting go!"

"Look!" yelled the prince, nodding back over his shoulder and kicking his feet. "Here comes that ghost again!"

No fury known to man could equal that which played across the distorted face of the ghost of Buckholly Harbor. She was done with talking, done with coaxing, done with all but killing. She sped like a gray comet toward the helpless pair, stretching her sword forward to its greatest reach, shrieking with cold-blooded violence.

"Watch out!" warned Danny Ray. A pinnacle of sharp rock rose up in front of them—the Hopeful Maiden.

"We're going to hit!" cried the prince.

But the magical rope of thrillium had other ideas. It drew them upward. The prince gasped. He raised his legs as high as he could. It would be a close call! Up they went—the prince's polka-dot robe just brushing over the top of the monument.

There the ghost of Buckholly Harbor stopped and hovered in midair; there she had reached the very edge of her domain, of her influence, of her power. For of old it was commanded her: The Hopeful Maiden is thy boundary; thus far, and only thus far shalt thou go.

She had been cheated again of her prey, and her maniac scream pursued Danny Ray and the prince as *Winter Queen* fled over the horizon.

⇒ 22 ⇐

Breaking and Entering

 "Whoa!" shouted the cowboy as *Winter Queen* turned sharply and sailed eastward toward the rising sun. He and the prince were swept up high and away from the queen. As they reached the extreme outward limit of their pendulum motion, he looked back with detached fascination at the beautiful ship.

"Oh no!" warned the prince. "Oh no! Oh no!"

The wind hummed ominously in the rope as they began their lethal return swing. Danny Ray knew they were dead if they smashed into *Winter Queen*'s white marble wall! He had only one chance!

"Quick!" he yelled. "Swing hard left!"

The rope seemed to sense their predicament, for it raised them level with the queen's elaborately carved stern, where a beautifully fashioned statue of a woman held out a scepter, her severe face gazing out in warning to any that would dare follow.

Here they came! The prince let out a piercing scream as

189

Winter Queen's towering stern-cabin windows loomed in front of them. The cowboy just had time to curl up in a ball and shoot out his feet, his tough cowboy boots absorbing the shock.

CRASH!

Danny Ray's world exploded in a shower of bright lights and shattering glass.

BOOM!

He collided with a heavy chair. The prince landed squarely on top of him, accidentally driving his knee into the cowboy's stomach, knocking the wind out of him.

"I'm alive!" the prince said excitedly, standing up and pumping his fists in the air. "I did it! I did it!"

"Yeah," groaned the cowboy. "You sure did. I didn't think—" Danny Ray was still gasping for air. "I didn't think— we had a *ghost* of a chance!"

The prince burst into laughter, and soon Danny Ray joined him. The cowboy groaned as the prince helped him to his feet and brushed pieces of broken glass off his vest.

The wind whipped through the gaping hole in the stern windows as Danny Ray readjusted his cowboy hat and gathered up his rope. Spanning the width of the spacious stern cabin, a huge polished table reflected the glittering chandeliers swaying from a large ceiling beam.

The sound of hurrying feet pattered overhead.

"C'mon!" the cowboy said excitedly. They ran around the end of the table to a large ornate door. They grabbed the knob at the same time.

"I forgot," said the prince with mock seriousness. "I should never have to open a door for myself!"

Danny Ray smirked at him. "You saved my life back there. Otherwise Ol' Miss Ghosty woulda had me for breakfast."

"I saw you flying by!" replied the prince. "The end of the rope came right at me, gleaming blue, and it seemed to say 'Grab me!' So I did."

"Well," said Danny Ray, opening the door, "let's go see the mess we've got ourselves into!"

They wrenched the door open and scurried up a flight of stairs and out onto *Winter Queen*'s spacious upper deck, brilliantly white in the morning sunlight.

WHAP! An axe buried itself in the doorway near the cowboy's head. He dove to the side, pulling the prince with him.

The deck was in chaos. The small group of Hogs led by Hoodie Crow and Mr. Piper was being beaten back and hemmed in by the queen's kidnappers, a troop of red devils and bollhockers, wearing spiked helmets and lantern jaws. At their head stood an immense red devil, a hellwain, brandishing a long pitchfork.

Danny Ray's appearance had caused a sudden lull in the strife. The sides separated as the prince, his sword drawn, led the cowboy between the two simmering crews.

"Bollhockers!" cautioned the prince. "They're the ones who can suck your brains out though your nose!"

"Hello, Hoodie," said Danny Ray, with a casual salute to the first lieutenant, who held a massive cutlass in one hand and a dagger in the other, his black hair and horns glinting in the sun. "Sorry about *Minnow*, sir. Hello, Mr. Piper."

"Nice run with the ghost, Danny Ray," commented the master gunner. He had a dagger cut on his arm and was bleeding. "We seen you from up here—"

"Ah! Hold still!" shouted the devil with a bestial snarl, motioning silence with his pitchfork. He ran his blistering yellow eyes up and down the cowboy, taking in his hat and blue rope, his vest and chaps, his boots and spurs. "A wizard, ha?"

The cowboy crossed his arms and declared, "My name's Danny Ray. I'm from the Otherworld!"

The devils and bollhockers grumbled uneasily and took a step back. Only the tall hellwain held his ground. He glared savagely at the cowboy. "Don't matter none my way. Wizard or not wizard there's more of us from you! You blokes thought of my crews off gathering hobbleberries, ha?" He scowled. "Didn't to think we have brains keepin' our ship tight against boarders, ha? Now, lay your weapons!"

"I am the prince of Elidor!" sneered the prince. "Why don't you just try to take my sword!"

"Where the heck's your captain?" demanded Danny Ray, his hands on his hips.

"Me," the hellwain sneered back, his pointed red tail wriggling like a giant worm. "I'm captain, ha?"

A few of his crew chuckled gloomily.

"No you're not!" replied the cowboy hotly. "First off, you don't have a hat with one of those silly white feathers, and second, I happen to know your captain's a stocky feller with a full black beard."

"Cap'n done shaved!" remarked a sarcastic little black devil, which brought a raucous chorus of chuckles from the crew. But in the devil's steely demeanor and in the laughter of the crew was an unmistakable quality of nervousness.

Suddenly there came a thunderous flapping of wings— WHUMMMF! WHUMMMF! WHUMMMF! A hideous pug-nosed face with sharp ears rose up over the queen's rim. The huge, leather-winged beast perched there, shaky in the sunlight.

"Ai!" A bollhocker pointed. His white teeth unlocked and he cried out, "A red bat!"

"Gods save us!" grumped another.

In contrast, the solitary form that dismounted that winged beast was extremely beautiful. Her leather traveling clothes seemed at odds with a girl beautiful enough to be a queen or a princess. Her black hair was pulled back tightly, her intelligent eyes taking in the situation on the deck. She waved Moonskimmer away and the bat flew back to the dark recesses of *Hog*.

"I am the Sultana Sumferi Sar," she stated in a high voice.

"And me, ha! I'm the green and slimy croakin' King of Frogs!" sneered the hellwain. He nodded, and a company of bollhockers with long spears scurried to surround her.

As proof, the girl displayed the great signet ring of the North on her finger, bearing the likeness of a dancing tiger. The hellwain's jaw muscles tightened.

She winked at Danny Ray and then faced the hellwain. "I have something that you might find very interesting." She reached inside her cloak and pulled out a small crystal orb: the

Heart of Ildirim. The crew's eyes widened as they observed its flickering red light.

"That light is very significant," pointed out the sultana. "The Sarksa pirates are not far away."

The large red devil said thickly, "Liar!" But his face said otherwise.

"It's true," interjected Danny Ray, putting up two fingers. "Scout's honor!"

"Ha?" growled a large bollhocker holding a two-headed axe.

"You consider the Sarksa pirates your allies because you both serve the same master—King Dru-Mordeloch." The sultana gave the hellwain a cold stare, and then peered out over a sea of bollhockers' and devils' horns. "But how can you, any of you, be sure the pirates won't murder you and take credit for recapturing *Winter Queen*?"

"This gets worse and worser!" said one weak-kneed bollhocker to his mate.

"What'll we do now?" grumbled another.

"We're done for it, that's what!" snapped a devil, licking his lips with a red tongue. "We'll boil—all in the same pot— together!"

A chorus of angry, confused voices broke out.

"Ah! Shut yer gobs!" barked the red devil, baring his fangs.

"I'm demanding you surrender this here queen!" said Danny Ray firmly.

"Ha!" The hellwain smirked, the scar on the side of his crimson face twitching. "You, demanding me?"

Just then, *Winter Queen*'s lookout cried a warning. Here

came *Hog* blasting out of the morning mist, having escaped
the harbor. She gained quickly on the queen.

Danny Ray had never once taken his eyes off the hellwain,
and he said evenly, "Surrender to us and live. Or to the Sarksa
pirates and find out what a nice bunch of fellers they really
are! Which is it gonna be?"

Several of the queen's crew didn't bother waiting for an order. The deck clattered noisily as they flung down their pikes
and clubs, their hatchets and maces. Others weren't so sure,
and they gripped their weapons nervously.

"You can't outrun the pirates," reasoned the sultana, guess-
ing the officer's thoughts. "Sooner or later they'll find you."

The red devil rubbed his chin with long, knotty fingers and
then came to loom over Danny Ray. The prince pointed his
blade directly at the chest of the hellwain, who called out to
two of his crew, "Jonesy! Chipper! Haul you down the flag.
Up helm! All engines stop!"

He unclasped his sword, offered it to the cowboy, and said
dully, "My sword you have!"

There arose a growl of reluctant approval from the rest of
his crew. *Winter Queen* slowed to a stop.

"Where's the real captain?" asked Danny Ray.

"Ah! I run from the harbor for it!" said the hellwain. "Left
my captain and half all the crews back in Buckholly's harbor."

Hog was close now, her cheering crew crowding her deck.
And since *Winter Queen* was so much taller than *Hog*, gang-
ways were thrown down from the rook's top deck to the middle deck of the queen.

As the prisoners were led below and the deck cleared,

Danny Ray was struck by the beauty of the queen's deck, her brass speaking tubes, her crystal top-knob and expensive gold gilding around the base of the main dome where the beautifully carved steerage wheel was located—and cannons! Danny Ray was surprised to see several massive brass cannons glinting in the sunlight.

"Danny Ray!" cried Captain Quigglewigg with a beaming face. He walked briskly across the deck followed by a crowd of Hogs to help man *Winter Queen*. He shook Danny Ray's hand in the morning light and said, "I give you joyous congratulations on your capture!"

"You'd better include the sultana and the prince." The cowboy smiled. "And Hoodie Crow and Mr. Piper!"

"Danny Ray!" laughed the sultana. "Listen!"

They peered down from the queen's lofty rim to *Hog*'s deck, crowded with every man jack aboard, Black Harry and Bulldog Jenkins among them, yelling and waving their weapons.

"I can hardly believe it!" exclaimed the cowboy, studying the devil's sword, the golden hilt, and the finely decorated scabbard. "*We* have captured *Winter Queen*!" With a smile he handed it to the prince and smiled warmly at Her Highness and stated, "I couldn't have done it without you guys!"

❧ 23 ❧

Checkmate

 Winter Queen and *Hog* sailed eastward at a crisp thirty knots with the Silverlode Mountains towering to the north. Hoodie Crow, telescope in hand, called out, "Signal from *Hog*: *Enemy in sight to the south'ard!*"

In a flash Danny Ray trained a telescope to starboard while the big first lieutenant sent a signal boy scampering to acknowledge *Hog*'s message. The cowboy sighed, handing the glass to the sultana.

" 'Fraid the magic stone was right," said Hoodie Crow, focusing his own telescope. "It's our ol' pirate friends, *Gallovidian*, *Sannox Bay*, and *Black Widow*—and they added another rook, a big one: the *Diamond*, an eighty-four-gunner."

It wasn't long before *Hog* sent another message: *Increase speed and continue on present course. Good luck!*

The prince frowned. "What does the captain mean, 'Good luck'?"

The coal-troll sucked his teeth and turned his hawk nose toward the prince. "Quiggs is ordering us to escape."

"But he won't have a chance against them four pirate ships!" said Danny Ray.

"He's sacrificing himself," realized the sultana.

Hog had slowed and prepared to turn south to meet the Sarksa pirates: alone. Already she was falling far behind.

"King Krystal—he's got to have his queen, right, Danny Ray?" asked Hoodie Crow gruffly. "I mean, that's the whole reason you're on this quest!"

"But we can't just leave Captain Quigglewigg to die, not after all he's done!" insisted the cowboy. "Turn this here ship around. Now!"

Hoodie laughed deeply. "I'm proud of you, Danny Ray!"

Hog and *Winter Queen* withdrew together northward and waited just off the coast where the Silverlode Mountains marched down to the Checkered Sea. The pirate ships stood off, positioning themselves to control any possible diagonals and files that *Winter Queen* could use for escape. The pirates had the advantage in men, in numbers, and in cannons.

When the sun had climbed to its zenith, *Black Widow*, once again bearing the commodore's pennant, which flew above a white flag of truce, left the squadron of pirates and sailed toward *Winter Queen*.

"Dang!" muttered Danny Ray under his breath as the pirate ship approached.

Hog inched forward a square to protect *Winter Queen*. *Black Widow* could not be up to any mischief, for her position was extremely vulnerable, leaving her open to a raking fire from the former garbage vessel.

"Signal from *Black Widow*," said Hoodie Crow. *"Permission to come aboard."*

The cowboy took off his hat and scratched his head. "Well, I reckon we should hear what they got to say. But we should allow only one pirate aboard, Hoodie."

The prince turned pale and fidgeted nervously with the hilt of his sword.

Soon, a crude rope bridge stretched from the top of *Black Widow* to *Winter Queen*'s lower crown. Walking on this shaky bridge posed no problems for the nimble, spidery form wearing a commodore's crimson cape. He stepped onto *Winter Queen*'s deck.

"Steady," said Danny Ray. The prince was sweating profusely as the rest of the Hogs fled the deck.

Danny Ray had forgotten how tall the Sarksa commodore was, almost ten feet, and the horrible sound his jaws made as they ground together. The cowboy held his breath. The side of the commodore's face had been burned badly—he had not escaped *Clackmannon*'s destruction unscathed. His honeycombed eyes considered them, but the commodore did not venture forward; clearly he didn't want to be perceived as hostile. The only visible sign of malice was his loathsome stinger, twitching with temper, and the long, curved sword hanging from his belt.

The commodore said with a thin voice, "Meet. Again."

"What do you want?" asked Danny Ray, folding his arms.

"Time. Is."

"Time for what?"

There was a pause. "Surrender." The jaws clicked menacingly. "You. Kowsboy. Prince man. Ssssultana. Ship. Others. Free."

"Remember what Piper said about the Sarksa," said the sultana in a shaky voice. "They'll torture us to death!"

"And *Winter Queen*—she'll be the commodore's," muttered Hoodie Crow. "Good day's work in any pirate's book!"

"Doggone it!" said the cowboy miserably. "We just captured this dang queen!"

The commodore took an instinctive step forward, one of hungry anticipation, much like a spider feeling a disturbance in its web after feeling the vibration given off by a panicked victim.

But then the Sarksa pirate's eyes narrowed as Danny Ray stood in front of the sultana and the prince and displayed his cutlass.

"We're in this together, Danny Ray," said Hoodie Crow, coming to stand beside him, gripping a boarding axe, and patting the flat of the head against his open palm.

"Ship there!" cried *Winter Queen*'s lookout.

Her Highness gripped the cowboy's arm.

The commodore wheeled and looked out over the sparkling marble expanse of the Checkered Sea. His antennae twitched and then he smiled triumphantly.

A groan of misery and despair went up from *Winter Queen*'s crew below deck. A black queen sailed swiftly over the horizon. The flag she flew: the skull and crossbones.

"Another pirate!" Hoodie Crow said mournfully. "Checkmate." He shook his great horned head, a note of resigned despair in his voice. "She's huge—look at her fly! She must mount over a hundred and thirty guns!"

"Why isn't she slowing down?" asked the sultana.

"Probably trying to impress her commodore," replied Danny Ray.

"Wait! She's accelerating!" said the sultana, her brown eyes widening.

"She's coming in too fast!" shouted the prince.

"She's going to ram us!" cried Danny Ray. "Quick! Grab on to something!"

The commodore sprang for safety, clinging to one of the spikes on the queen's crown, his long, spidery arms black against the queen's white pureness. But there was no such place of escape for Danny Ray and his friends.

With a roar the black queen blazed past *Winter Queen*. With full force she collided with *Black Widow*, smashing her to pieces right in front of the commodore's eyes! The bishop's smoking pedestal careered away lopsidedly, wobbling out to strike *Diamond* a terrible blow, ripping a deep gash in the heavy rook's starboard side.

The pirate queen, shimmering with power, sat right next to *Winter Queen* on the exact square the pirate bishop occupied. She was a replica of *Winter Queen* except that she was pitch black, so black that she shone with a purplish hue, undoubtedly the reason for the name LADY AMETHYST scrolled across her stern.

"Danny Ray!" The sultana pointed. *Lady Amethyst*'s pirate

flag fluttered down, replaced by a flag bearing a white crown on a field of purple.

"Hello, Your Highness!" boomed a familiar voice. Gimmion Gott, huge and resplendent in a sparkling officer's uniform, saluted from *Lady Amethyst's* deck.

"Where did you get that queen, Gimmion?" called out the sultana in an astonished voice.

"This be the black queen of King Krystal's, Your Highness!" yelled back Gimmion. "Come into Port Palnacky just two days gone now, looking for the white queen! What speed! What verve! Look at these cannons! There be more than a hundred of 'em!"

"Pleasant to see you alive, Danny Ray!" came a new voice. Captain Shimmersheen appeared at the black queen's raked rim and waved along with a host of Elidor's cheering men.

"Howdy, Captain!" said Danny Ray, touching the rim of his hat.

"Captain! Gimmion, please!" The sultana pointed to *Hog*, sailing bravely out to do battle with *Gallovidian* and *Sannox Bay*. "Go help Captain Quigglewigg. Go help *Hog*!"

Captain Shimmersheen saluted and *Lady Amethyst* sped off.

❧ 24 ❧

Fight to the Death!

 Danny Ray caught a sparkle at the corner of his eye, the glittering edge of a sword flashing toward his head—just time to duck as *whooooosh!* it passed over.

He had forgotten about the Sarksa commodore!

The cowboy's world jerked upside down as he was pushed against the rim, and then he grunted as the sultana landed on top of him. Danny Ray jumped up. Hoodie Crow had pushed them both clear of danger. The first lieutenant gripped his axe, squaring off with the commodore.

The commodore circled, hissing, sizing up the coal-troll. His drawn sword glinted. The air sizzled as he pulled out a black dagger, gleaming like obsidian. His barbs, as sharp as knives, jutted out of each shoulder. Spittle bubbled about his jaws.

"Stay here!" said Danny Ray to the sultana as he retrieved a cutlass lying on the deck.

Hoodie rushed at the commodore, swinging his axe, and the commodore barely parried his thunderous downswing.

The Sarksa swung his dagger at Hoodie's ducking head and then kicked savagely at the troll, sending him backward over a pile of heavy cannonballs, to hit his head with a resounding *dong!* against one of the *Winter Queen*'s massive brass cannons.

Hoodie lay motionless.

The commodore spun around, searching, locking his eyes on to the cowboy. Danny Ray backpedaled, holding up his cutlass while he groped for his magic rope. The sun passed behind a cloud, making the commodore seem that much darker, loom that much larger as he approached the cowboy.

Swisssssh! The commodore swung his sword and kicked a barbed foot at Danny Ray's head, and then lunged with his dagger, but the cowboy backed away.

Again he attacked and again Danny Ray fell back, drawing the pirate farther and farther away from the sultana, who knelt over Hoodie Crow.

Danny shot a look around the deck. Where was the prince?

The cowboy ducked under another swishing sword stroke and danced backward. The commodore hesitated as Danny Ray began twirling his rope and said, "Come on, you big bug. Come get what's coming to you!"

The commodore attacked and Danny Ray threw the rope, snagging the black dagger and wrenching it out of the pirate's hand, sending the weapon clattering into the scuppers.

Repeatedly the commodore lunged with his sword, backing Danny Ray around the deck into the shadow of *Winter Queen*'s center knob. The cowboy panted. He tripped the pirate with a well-aimed toss of the rope and went to slash down with his cutlass, but the commodore nimbly rolled away and then sprang to his feet.

Danny Ray's sword met the commodore's sword full speed, edge-to-edge, and the cowboy's cutlass flew out of his hand, clanging over toward the steerage wheel, where a certain prince trembled.

"Prince!" screamed the sultana. She had gotten Hoodie Crow, groggy and bleary-eyed, to a sitting position. "You must help Danny Ray!"

The cowboy lunged to one side as the commodore slashed with his sword but missed. Danny Ray scooted along the wall until he felt the cold brass of a cannon against his back. WHANG! Danny Ray twisted out of the way as the Sarksa's barbed foot kicked against the big forty-two pounder.

The cowboy found himself pinned against the wall. The pirate paused, laughing, his inner fangs separating to reveal a jagged tongue. As his hand involuntarily touched his scarred face, his laughter ceased, turning into volcanic rage.

"Time. Die."

Down came the Sarksa's sword. Danny Ray just had the strength to hold up his rope with both hands and blunt the stroke. Danny Ray fell to his hands and knees and scampered beneath the huge cannon and out the other side. The prince still cringed at the wheel, Danny Ray's cutlass lying at his feet.

"Help!" Danny Ray called. "Prince, help—or it's all over!"

The shadow of the Sarksa loomed over him. The pirate grunted as he swung his sword downward. Back beneath the cannon Danny rolled, the steel blade of the pirate sending up a shower of splinters from the deck.

"Help," he gasped. His arms trembled as he hunched over. No strength left. He panted heavily, waited, waited, but the commodore never appeared.

Danny Ray saw why: The Prince had left the cutlass but had drawn his own sword, facing off with the commodore! Surprisingly, it was the prince who attacked.

He can't fight him all alone! thought Danny Ray as he hauled himself up on a pair of wobbly legs. He's going to get himself killed!

The Sarksa hissed and recoiled from the prince. He heaved his stinger up behind his head in a threatening posture that had disabled many of his enemies out of sheer terror. He viciously attacked the prince, again and again, the prince backing up against the steerage wheel.

The commodore had his back turned to the cowboy. *Whooooosh! Whooooosh! Whooooosh!* went Danny Ray's rope. He let it fly. It looped down over the pirate's head and gripped his neck.

The commodore jerked over, grabbing at his throat. "Whoa!" cried Danny Ray as he was catapulted off his feet into the air. The rope hauled the cowboy up the commodore's back. Danny Ray draped his legs over his shoulders, just inside the cruel spikes.

"You wanted me, Mr. Commodore," challenged Danny Ray as the pirate bucked this way, lunged that way. "Now you've got me!"

Danny Ray hung on for dear life. The commodore couldn't shake the cowboy. He tried slashing back with his sword but only injured himself. Danny Ray stuck like flypaper, kicking his spurs again and again against the Sarksa's chest. He rode him hard, his right hand waving in the air for balance, his left gripping the blue rope wrapped tightly around the pirate's throat.

"Ah!" groaned Danny Ray. He felt a sharp, stabbing pain in the middle of his back. He had forgotten about the Sarksa's stinger!

Unexpectedly, the commodore let out a horrible shriek. He fell and rolled over, grasping his side, and Danny Ray was thrown violently into the scuppers. The prince had moved in on the preoccupied pirate and had struck him with his sword.

"Enough!" the commodore gurgled with intense pain and anger, and rose to his feet, holding his side. His breath hissed like steam as it issued out of his mouth.

But the prince walked confidently, almost casually toward the commodore, a fell light shining in his eyes. He grunted as he struck like lightning with his sword. The Sarksa parried and fell back. Again and again the prince attacked, fearless, swinging his blade with pent-up wrath.

"No!" shrieked Danny Ray, his heart leaping into his throat.

The prince slowed to stop. He had rushed recklessly once too often at the commodore, whose stinger, dripping with milky-white poison, had struck swiftly, deeply into his shoulder.

The prince took a deep breath and lowered to one knee,

resting his arm on his sword's hilt. The Sarksa's eyes narrowed as he came to stand over him—young fool!

The cowboy shook his blurry head. Off to the side something gleamed on the deck—the pirate's black dagger! Danny Ray groped and then closed his fingers around its handle. He wiped at his eyes; the poison was beginning to take effect. He winced and shielded his eyes against the deck, snowy white in the sunlight. He choked back a sob as the Sarksa commodore struck the prince again with his stinger. Even now the poison would be coursing through his royal veins, flowing to his failing heart.

Armed with the dagger, Danny Ray sprang wearily at the commodore. His legs dragged like lead. Just as the commodore lifted his sword over the prince for the kill, Danny Ray struck with the last of his strength, stabbing down through the Sarksa's foot with such force that the dagger stuck fast in the wooden deck.

Danny Ray collapsed onto his back. The commodore laid back his black head against the blue sky and roared, his jaws working back and forth in an excruciating frenzy. He reached down, grabbing the dagger's handle.

It wouldn't budge.

"Smile!" shouted Hoodie Crow.

The huge first lieutenant had swiveled a large brass cannon and aimed it directly at the commodore. The commodore froze, nailed in place by the dagger. Then he smiled sickly.

"This is for our lookout!" cried Hoodie Crow.

The sultana, a revengeful smile playing across her lips, lowered a slow match over the cannon's touchhole.

Just as the commodore dislodged the dagger and raised it triumphantly in the air, the cannon vomited forth a long orange flame followed by a loud BOOM! A forty-two-pound iron cannonball, hot and humming, with a circular halo hovering about it, blazed across the deck like an avenging meteor.

The commodore was blasted into bits.

Danny Ray opened his dry mouth, and said slowly, "Stone. Cold. Dead."

The cowboy was fading fast—the sky, the clouds, blurring. He felt the sultana's breath against his cheek, her urgent, hysterical voice in his ear. Someone else raised his head. A face materialized out of the mist: the prince, with fierce eyes like a lion. As he brought his hand against Danny Ray's wound, the cowboy felt a glowing sensation spreading from his back over his whole body. Unexplainably, his strength returned, and he sat up, dazed.

"How in tarnation did you do that?" Danny Ray asked the prince. "I thought you were dead!"

The prince got to his feet. He seemed to have grown in stature, his robe having miraculously changed to a fresh, vibrant blue.

"What the heck happened to the prince?" asked Danny Ray, under his breath. "Or should I say, Prince Blue?"

The sultana stared with openmouthed amazement.

It was dusk by the time Danny Ray was fit enough to find his way to *Winter Queen*'s deck. The powerful black queen, *Lady Amethyst*, trailed in their wake. The wind played dreamily in the cowboy's hair and he yawned, a deep, jaw-splitting yawn. A shooting star blazed overhead, passing from the constellation of the Jester to that of the Emperor, and then faded out over the horizon.

Voices came from the front rim where Prince Blue and the sultana stood with one another. She handed something sparkly to the prince as the cowboy walked up.

"Hello, Danny Ray!" cried Prince Blue. On his finger was a new gold ring.

"So, you gave him your signet ring, Your Highness," stated Danny Ray flatly.

"Yes," she replied, biting her lip. "But here!" she said, holding out the small jeweled orb. "You may have the Heart of Ildirim!"

Danny Ray's heart sank just a little, but shucks, he had to admit they'd be a good match. The sultana was a classy girl, nearly a princess herself. And the prince, well, he seemed almost like a king now.

"Danny Ray, you're looking at me so strangely!" Prince Blue frowned. "I haven't changed that much!"

"You gotta be kiddin'!" laughed the cowboy.

They fell silent for a time, looking out over the squares flying rapidly beneath them as *Winter Queen* hummed along at a fantastic speed.

The cowboy yawned again. "Time to turn in. I'm dog-tired! Goodnight, Your Highness. Goodnight, Prince . . . Blue."

"Goodnight, Danny Ray," they said

He dragged his feet across the deck toward the stairs leading below, to his cabin and a warm bed. But then he paused and glanced back at the prince, the new stars of night circling his head. Prince Blue. Yeah, that title fit him just right!

❖ 25 ❖

A Homecoming

 In a small shrine laden with drooping flowers, King Krystal knelt, eyes closed. This day promised to be the blackest in his life, even darker than the day his wife, the late queen of Elidor, had died. He sighed and looked out over Birdwhistle Bay with its beautiful harbor entrance guarded by the Tower of the Rose and the Tower of Fire.

A figure with a long, angular white beard came and stood nearby: Lord Chessboard. Dressed in a towering black headdress and flowing robes displaying a chessboard pattern, he resembled a black-and-white hourglass. He had just arrived to ensure that the rules of the Great Chess Game were strictly enforced.

"Hello, old friend." King Krystal smiled. With a great effort the king braced himself against his silver cane and stood, shaking his hand. "Well met!"

"Any news of the cowboy?" asked Lord Chessboard.

"He is dead," King Krystal said wearily.

"Pity. What of the prince?" Lord Chessboard inquired, his gray eyes showing a spark of interest.

"Don't know." The king shook his head. "I armed the black queen, *Lady Amethyst*, with cannons and sent her out. I should have thought of it sooner! But where *Lady Amethyst* is now, I have no clue."

"Again, pity," said Lord Chessboard.

"Yes, a great pity," replied the king. "Poor little Princess Amber hasn't slept for days. She has cried and cried to think that soon she will become wed to Dru-Mordeloch!"

"Pearls before swine, surely," said Lord Chessboard.

Scragtail, the little gossip, perched nearby. Its striped hide blended perfectly with the patterns of light and shadow inside the shrine. The gossip scratched behind one large ear with its sharp, jeweled tail. But then it raised its head, large ears quivering. In a flash, it flitted out over the garden toward the bay and disappeared.

"Ah!" said the king, raising his arms. "What will Birdwhistle Bay look like after Dru-Mordeloch pulls down its fine walls and towers, uproots its gardens and ancient trees? And what will come of my precious daughter, pure, innocent Amber with the golden hair and lilting laughter? She will surely die within the year after being forced to wed such a tyrant."

A crowd of darkly robed figures congregated on the garden stairs. At their head stood King Dru-Mordeloch of Trowland, tall and imposing. Even at that distance King Krystal could see his bloodred eyes. His robes were black for the occasion (for on this day he was to play the black pieces), as were his horns, neatly polished and set with sparkling gems. His dark consorts laughed among themselves at King Krystal's terrible plight.

The sparkling crystal crown of Elidor, studded with sapphires and pearls, glinted on King Krystal's brow in the morning sun. He said, "I still have until noontime."

"Yes, by law you do," intoned Lord Chessboard, "at which time you must forfeit the chess game, and with it, your crown, your kingdom, and your daughter, to Dru-Mordeloch. As great a chess master as you are, Your Majesty, you would have no chance playing Dru-Mordeloch without your queen. And by law you cannot set the pieces on the board, even by depriving Dru-Mordeloch of his black queen by sailing her away."

King Krystal brought up his hand beneath his chin and voiced his first doubts: "Ah! I should have known Danny Ray was not experienced enough for so great a task! I let my anger control me by sending the prince along as his companion! What a fool I was!" King Krystal tapped his cane lightly on the stone floor. "Why did the Lord Advocate send one so unpracticed as Danny Ray? It doesn't make sense! Now the brave young warrior from the Otherworld is dead, and Elidor is doomed!"

"It is one thing to call oneself a fool," said Lord Chessboard, compassion mixed with caution in his voice, "and quite another to question the Lord Advocate."

"Yes, of course you're right," said King Krystal with a wave of his hand.

Bing-bong! Bing-bong! Bing-bong!

Bells began ringing! But not fire bells, not bells of warning, not lonely bells of mourning, but bells so bright, bells of delight! But on such a hopeless day, who could be celebrating?

"Father!" Princess Amber skipped to King Krystal, her blond hair bouncing off her shoulders. She seized the king's hand and twirled in a joyous pirouette, her dress spinning and rustling merrily like dry autumn leaves. "Oh father! The queen! She has returned!"

Lovely in the morning haze of the Checkered Sea, out beyond the boundaries of Birdwhistle Bay, there approached an immensely tall white tower with sharp spikes at her crown. She grew larger by the minute, escorted from behind into Birdwhistle Bay by another queen, black and elegant.

It must be a dream! The king could hardly believe his eyes! Yes! *Winter Queen's* details were more pronounced as she dropped anchor. Cheering multitudes rushed toward the bay as King Krystal shouted for joy!

"Father, the flowers!" exclaimed the princess as one by one, blossom by blossom, the wilted flowers trailing about the shrine's latticework began to revive. Red dragon-fires flamed to life, bouquets of love-in-the-mist blossoms raised their weary heads, while fairy cups opened their brilliant blue petals and smiled at the king. Even the trees groaned, straightening up from their drooping posture.

A scowling King Dru-Mordeloch approached King Krystal and smoke went up from that dark ruler like the smoke from a furious furnace. All of his dark plans unraveled before his eyes. In but a moment the kingdom of Elidor and lovely Princess Amber had slipped from his grasp.

"King Krystal," said Dru-Mordeloch wrathfully. "You have not heard the last of me in regard to this humiliation. This world is with dark powers filled, full of envious and formidable spirits in strife versed. Beware. For I shall marshal talents extraordinary, in arts magical, and visit you another season. I say to you, King Krystal, beware of Dru-Mordeloch!"

"I take it, then, the Great Chess Game is canceled?" inquired King Krystal with a mischievous twinkle in his eye.

Princess Amber tilted her head and laughed with the same ringing tone as that of the merry-bells that still floated over the cheering inhabitants of Elidor.

"Not the last!" promised Dru-Mordeloch with a final furious flurry of his cape. The king of Trowland floated up the stairs and disappeared.

"Aha!" Amber cried, snapping her little fingers at Dru-Mordeloch's departing entourage.

"Aha!" chimed in the king.

Scragtail flitted back from Birdwhistle Bay and circled overhead, crying, "Lives, Danny Ray! Lives, Danny Ray!"

Lord Chessboard's normally stern face broke out into a grin. King Krystal danced and danced and danced, his crown tilting down over one eye, and he laughed and laughed and laughed.

"I knew Danny Ray was the right choice all along—never a doubt in my mind!" panted King Krystal. But the princess gave him a sidelong glance. "Well . . . maybe I doubted him a trifle, but what do I care now? *Winter Queen* has been returned!"

✴ 26 ✴

Fare You Well

The captain of the mumpokers stood before the great doors of Grand Hall, from which Danny Ray and the prince had set out two weeks before. Wild rumors as to the identity of the strange and exotic crew members of *Winter Queen* and *Lady Amethyst* bubbled among the expectant crowd, packed elbow-to-elbow in the hall.

King Krystal and Princess Amber waited on the dais at the far end of the hall. Three times the mumpoker pounded the marble floor with his staff, BOOM! BOOM! BOOM!, and announced, "The commander of *Hog*, Captain Quigglewigg; first lieutenant, Mr. Hoodie Crow; gunner of the ship, Mr. Piper!"

The great doors opened and raucous applause echoed off the walls. Three officers walked down the main aisle: Captain Quigglewigg, wearing his finest white breeches and black boots topped off by a beautiful blue waistcoat with bright gold buttons; Hoodie Crow, the huge and hulking coal-troll with the downturned horns, having taken the time to varnish his wooden leg; Mr. Piper, smiling like the sun, his arm back in a

217

sling and his gray pigtail decorated with a black ribbon. The master gunner bowed this way and that to the crowd, as if he had single-handedly captured *Winter Queen!*

BOOM! BOOM! BOOM!

"Her Highness, from Palnacky Roads! The Sultana Sumferi Sar!" Applause again, and reverent bows from the crowd. The diminutive sultana, still in her traveling clothes and cloak, dwarfed by the ponderous purple giant, Gimmion Gott, waved back to the crowd on her way to the dais.

BOOM! BOOM! BOOM!

"Prince Blue!" The applause was somewhat scattered, confused, as an unknown boy strode forward to the dais. His lantern jaw was stern, and neither to the right nor left did he gaze, but steadily forward to the king and his daughter, who regarded him with wonder.

What amazing thing had happened to the prince? The blue of his robes was dazzling, like that of a summer sky. Rumor was that the sword at his side had struck down a thousand Sarksa pirates!

"The commander of *Lady Amethyst*, Captain Shimmersheen!" Amid the applause, Lord Red and Lord Green with other members of the court studied the captain with narrow, suspicious eyes.

BOOM! BOOM! BOOM!

The captain of the mumpokers' chest expanded as he said, "Last but not least! It is my duty. It is my honor. It is my privilege to present: The rodeo cowboy from Tahlequah, Oklahoma! Danny Ray!"

The cowboy appeared, holding the white cage with the two

golden clabbernappers chattering noisily to the crowd. He walked shyly toward the dais amid a rush of applause. A colorful flurry of confetti descended on him. Faces flashed at him, outstretched hands, the people jumping around like popcorn!

Danny Ray smiled at Captain Shimmersheen and Captain Quigglewigg and his officers, who stood off to one side, and then bowed politely to the sultana, Gimmion, and Prince Blue. He climbed the elegantly carpeted stairs, slipped off his cowboy hat, and lowered himself to his knees before the king. Scragtail's tiny form flitted down onto the cowboy's shoulder, turning black against his leather vest.

The hall fell quiet.

"Rise, Danny Ray!" commanded King Krystal.

Princess Amber approached the cowboy. He set aside the clabbernappers as she reached out to hold both of his hands. She looked shyly at him and said: "Danny Ray, two weeks ago you left this very hall with a charge: Return *Winter Queen* in time for the Great Chess Game. Although we wish to goodness you had not taken all of the time allotted"—there followed a smattering of good-natured tittering—"you succeeded admirably. You have saved Elidor, and me!"

Danny Ray could only nod, staring back into her sparkling gray eyes.

The king cleared his throat. "Furthermore, Danny Ray, in recognition and appreciation of what you have accomplished, I find it impossible to withhold from you anything that you might ask of me. My treasury and my kingdom are open to you!"

The crowd held its breath. King Krystal was extremely wealthy; Danny Ray had been offered a fortune! Scragtail nodded its head up and down emphatically and croaked out his approval.

"I'd like to say, sir," announced Danny Ray, "that without all the folks standing up here, there's no way I could have rescued your queen—especially without these here clabbernappers!"

The cowboy lifted the white cage and a fresh wave of applause erupted, threatening to shatter the delicate windows.

With that, the celebration began.

Glasses of cherrymaine were clinked together. Great tables were wheeled into the hall laden with one hundred and twenty plates of cheeses and artichokes; forty immense platters piled with fruit tarts; one hundred and seventy chickens—some baked with orange chutney, others with tomatoes and rosemary; nineteen elegant swans roasted in their own feathers; and fifteen huge pickled pigs (one very large pig encircled by a moat of cranberry marmalade), all of them arranged reverently kneeling, like pilgrims, around a fountain of magnificent raspberry champagne.

"As far as gifts, Your Majesty," said Danny Ray over the hullabaloo of the crowd. "Shoot, I wish Captain Quigglewigg could get a whole new rook! His old ship, *Hog*, is pretty beat up."

"Thank you, Danny Ray!" beamed Captain Quigglewigg. "Like I said—you're my favorite landlubber!"

"Also, if it wouldn't be asking too much, sir," continued Danny Ray, "I'd like to throw a big party for Prince Blue to celebrate his change in color!"

"Indeed!" said King Krystal with raised eyebrows. "He's become a grand fellow, has he not? Never thought I'd see such a change in him! Lord Chessboard will be interested in his improvement."

Danny Ray met the sultana's eyes, and she gave the smallest shake of her head. She needed no gifts or recognition, being very wealthy herself. Her reward had been in the adventure of helping to rescue *Winter Queen*.

The light through the windows played softly on the cowboy's face, a lonely, tired face.

Princess Amber asked, "Danny Ray, why do you look so sad? You just saved all of Elidor! How can my father reward you?"

"I'd like to head on home. Back to Oklahoma. I miss my mom, and I miss my dad, and I miss my brothers, and I miss my dog."

The king mirrored his sad face. "I'm sorry, Danny Ray. If it were in my power to send you home, I would gladly do so!"

Scragtail sensed something strange, calling out a warning.

"Watch out!" warned Princess Amber, pulling Danny Ray close to herself. The sultana frowned. Everyone stopped eating and drinking, breathing and blinking, talking and thinking! A glimmering, shimmering square floated down to the dais. It straightened on end, its surface wavering like water, reflecting splashes of light off the polished stairs.

"Well, Danny Ray," said the king. "Your wish to go home has been granted!"

Danny Ray suddenly felt very awkward.

Captain Quigglewigg stepped forward and shook the cowboy's hand. "Danny Ray, you must visit us again and come sailing with me! After all, you helped defeat *Vulture*, *Clackmannon*, *Wick*, and *Black Widow*!" The captain wrapped his arm around the cowboy's shoulder and his orange face lit up with a grin. "Oh—did I tell you? I made another joke! Let me see, oh yes! Capturing *Winter Queen* is your crowning achievement—ha, ha! Did you catch it, *crowning* achievement? What a regal fellow I am—oh, ha, ha, ha!"

"And, Danny Ray," added Hoodie Crow in a gravelly voice, thumping forward. "You outwitted the Sarksa queen!"

"And you outfoxed the ghost of Buckholly Harbor!" chimed in Mr. Piper.

"And you roped *Winter Queen* and then captured her!" smiled Prince Blue.

"*Helped* capture her," emphasized Danny Ray warmly. "I wasn't the only one who crashed through her stern windows!"

"You smashed her windows?" King Krystal gasped, completely dismayed.

"We're putting a fix to 'em now, Your Kinglyship," said Mr. Piper, knuckling his forehead before he could catch himself.

Captain Quigglewigg and his crew stepped aside to make room for the purple giant, who lumbered up before the cowboy—alone.

"Where—where did the sultana go?" the cowboy asked. "I need to say goodbye."

"The sultana are gone, Danny Ray," said the purple giant, a sudden look of sadness crossing his face. "She saw the magic doorway and knew you are to go home. It are sometimes the way of the world that the things most precious to us be the very treasures we cannot hold. You, Danny Ray, must remain in her dreams," continued Gimmion softly, "as she hopes to remain in yours. We of Port Palnacky wish you luck and good fortune. Peace! Honor! Prosperity!"

Danny Ray frowned. Shoot, why was the sultana so upset about him leaving if she liked the prince? After all, she gave him her golden ring!

One last fellow stood forward who had come to mean a whole lot to Danny Ray. Robed in blue and toying with the hilt of his sword, Prince Blue settled his brown eyes on the cowboy. "I guess you're leaving, Danny Ray."

"Yeah," he replied uneasily, "I better get on back home." He wiped his nose with his sleeve. "But, heck, I'll miss this place, where bats are as big as dragons, and dragons are as big as bats!"

Prince Blue grabbed Danny Ray, hugging him close, and whispered in his ear, "I don't know exactly where Oklahoma is, but it will always be dear to my heart. You liked me when I was unlikable, Danny Ray, and I'll never forget you!"

Prince Blue held the cowboy so that he could look at him, and shook his hand one last time. Scragtail fluttered off Danny Ray's shoulder and onto the prince's, turning a vivid, bright blue.

Lord Chessboard, robed in black-and-white chess pattern, loomed up behind Prince Blue. Danny Ray remembered the prince's dream, the stern-faced man with a white beard, a black robe, and a high black crown. Lord Chessboard gently placed his hand on Prince Blue's shoulder, startling him. Prince Blue glanced down at his great signet ring and a worried look crossed his features. But then he relaxed, a confident air replacing his apprehension.

"Danny Ray," said the king in a serious tone, "I have learned an important lesson: Never doubt the ability of someone just because they're young and inexperienced! After hearing the wild stories of the rescue, only now do I understand the wisdom of the Lord Advocate, and why he sent you! Farewell, Danny Ray!"

The cowboy felt a lump form in his throat and he swallowed hard. It dawned on him: This was goodbye to his friends. He took one last look at Grand Hall, with its towering pillars, its colorful windows and lights, and at his Companions of the Quest.

Princess Amber smiled affectionately at the cowboy, and his heart jumped. She said mischievously, "You are always welcome within the borders of Elidor, Lord Cowboy."

"No, ma'am," said the cowboy with wet cheeks. He touched the rim of his hat. "The name's Danny Ray: And I'm the best dang rodeo cowboy in Oklahoma."